BLACK ACES

BLACK ACES

Stephen Payne

GUNSMOKE

This hardback edition 2009
by BBC Audiobooks Ltd
by arrangement with
Golden West Literary Agency

ISBN 978 1 405 68252 7

British Library Cataloguing in Publication Data available.

Printed and bound in Great Britain by
CPI Antony Rowe, Chippenham and Eastbourne

BLACK ACES

CHAPTER ONE

ELEVEN HORSES FOR ONE

There had been excitement and much talk in Swiftwater town of a rancher found mysteriously murdered with an ace of spades lying on his bullet-pierced breast. But young Tedro Ames had paid scant heed, for Sheriff Potter's business was of no concern to him.

Riding home from Swiftwater in the wee small hours, this carefree cowboy-rancher lifted his rich baritone voice to the night-prowling coyotes and the vast silent rangeland.

"Jack o' Diamonds, Jack o' Diamonds, I know you of old,
You've robbed my poor house of silver and gold."

He sang because in all this cattle land there was not a happier fellow than he, and the superb pinto pony he was leading had much more to do with this complacent mood than the liquor he had sampled in town.

Arrived at the small T A ranch, Tedro stabled his saddler and the pinto in the tumble-down shed which served as a barn, then sauntered across the starlit yard to his weather-beaten log cabin. As he lighted a lamp in the kitchen the cheap alarm clock on its shelf above the warped and rusty cook stove indicated 3 A.M.

7

Yet, regardless of the hour, of physical weariness and of sleep-hungry, blood-shot eyes, Tedro emptied his mail sack on the table and idled for a few minutes glancing at what it had contained. A livestock market circular and a saddle catalog he tossed aside; a square, pink envelope with typewritten address received a cursory glance, and then he unfolded a copy of the local newspaper—the *Swiftwater Star.*

On the back page of this Tedro's gaze roved down the "personals" and "The News From Various Sources." Often in the past eighteen months there had been items in these columns concerning one Tedro Ames, sometimes flattering, sometimes blunt to the point of cruelty. Editor Ray Thomas spoke his mind, spared no one. Ah, here was a barbed shaft:

"The enterprising young ranchman of Twisty Creek has sold one hundred cows and calves— the pick of his herd—to Frank R. Carter. Upon being interviewed by ye correspondent, Carter stated, in his usual dry manner, that he got a rare bargain.

"When this shrewd old cow thief—beg pardon, Frank—they say, jokingly, that whenever you buy a cow or a horse you steal it—says a bargain he means a bargain. What Tedro Ames, the seller, thinks we have not had the opportunity to inquire. But watch your step, Tedro."

A smile faintly derisive creased the corners of

Tedro's firm lips. Bold black type headed the next item to arrest his attention.

"ELEVEN GOOD HORSES FOR ONE!"

"Neighbor Greasy Holderness, smiling broadly to say the least, reports that at last he has parted with his wonder horse, Apache. It is rumored that a certain most attractive young woman has for long had her eye on this famous pinto—the only pinto saddler in all Swiftwater Valley. Therefore we drew some interesting conclusions when we learned from Mr. Holderness how two of our prominent young cowmen have—each unknown to the other—been dickering with Holderness for possession of Apache.

"However, Tedro Ames, the lucky dog, outbid Leonard M. Stoddard. The price? See heading of this item. But dirt cheap at that, all things considered, eh, Tedro?"

Tossing the newspaper in the general direction of the warped stove Tedro chuckled with whole-hearted delight. He never would forget the look on Len Stoddard's iron-jawed face when Stoddard accompanied by his brother, had seen him leading the pinto into Swiftwater at sundown last evening. But Leonard M. had only himself to blame for losing Apache. He was "too tight-fisted" to pay Holderness his price.

Tight-fisted? A goodly number of the Swiftwater

9

ranchers were afflicted that way, and Bill McKenzie was the tightest of them all. But that was to be expected of a canny old Scot. Bill McKenzie owned the best ranch in the valley and three thousand head of choice Hereford cattle. To please his daughter—the young woman mentioned by inference in the *Swiftwater Star*—he might have bought the pinto pony fifty times over and never missed the cash or its equivalent in stock. But had he done it? Oh, no. McKenzie would pay not a nickel more for anything than it was actually worth.

As for Tedro Ames, he now told himself that he had no such silly ideas of economy and thrift. When he wanted something he went after it and got it. In fancy he could see Fay McKenzie's alert blue eyes light with pleasure; her winsome face register sheer joy as he presented Apache to her. After this—

Abruptly the dream faded, for Tedro, mechanically opening the square, pink envelope, had drawn from it a playing card—the black ace of spades. Although not superstitious, this gave young Ames a queer apprehensive start. Nothing was written on the card; nothing else in the envelope. Why was some fool sending him an ace of spades? It seemed a pointless silly joke.

After a moment of finger-combing his hair, very black, very curly and as thick as a beaver's fur, Tedro shoved the card back in the envelope, laid it on the table, and then, as he glanced around the disorderly kitchen his attention suddenly focused upon the discarded newspaper. It lay on the cold stove, with the front page at which he had not looked, uppermost.

"RANCHER DRYGULCHED!"

Under this glaring headline:

"Early this morning Paul E. Smith was found in his own front yard, lying face up to the sun, lifeless. Smith had been shot in the back squarely between his shoulder blades with a high power rifle. Weighted down with a small rock on the dead cowman's breast was a playing card—the black ace of spades!"

Tedro's eyes flicked to the pink envelope. He shrugged, said: "Oh hell! Just a queer coincidence my gettin' a black ace. I recall talk in the saloon. Folks were bettin' Smith's neighbor, Sorenson, got him."

Resolutely the young ranchman picked up the lamp, entered his room, kicked off his boots and his trousers, blew out the light and settled down on his bunk.

Sometime later, Tedro was drowsily aware that Ike Bowlaigs looked in on him, muttered something into his saddle-colored mustache and went out abruptly, closing the door behind him.

Ike Bowlaigs was Tedro's one and only hired man. Once this veteran cowhand had been known as Bow-legged Ike, but that was long years ago when he had come up the trail from Texas with cowman Bill McKenzie, driving a thousand long-horned cows. Where what later became known as Trail Rest Creek flowed into the Swiftwater River, Bill McKenzie had stopped to rest his herd—and had stayed.

McKenzie had built up his longhorn herd at first with Durham bulls, later with Herefords; had built up also a splendid ranch, and what is perhaps more important he had sent to Bonny Scotland for the girl he'd left behind. Folks who should know said old Bill had hoped to have sons to carry on his business. But his only child was a girl. Such a girl as warmed the cockles of his staunch old heart however, and—though he did not say so—kept him worried for fear she would marry some "triflin', laz-zy whe-elp."

Bow-Legged Ike, who was old in those days when McKenzie was still a young man, had coddled Fay McKenzie on his warped and bony knees before she learned to walk, and afterwards. It was he who had first affectionately dubbed her "Sandy." In turn, it was this little sandy-haired freckled girl who had twisted his name around. To her he was always Ike Bowlaigs, at first to his dismay, later to his delight.

Ike was rated a good cowman, but McKenzie never made him foreman. He was too peppery of tongue, lacked that certain knack of handling men, especially the rough, tough men McKenzie was forced to hire in those early days, far from the railroad, far from the settlements. But to the old Half Moon outfit Ike was loyalty personified, and never had he been quite so disgruntled as upon the day when Sandy asked him to go and work for Tedro Ames.

"Huh? Huh? Gosh all tomahawks, gal! Yere I been with ol' Bill fer twenty odd year, an' you tried fer to bite my thumb the day after you was bornt. You mean I should quit an' go punch caows fer that lazy, hoss-swappin' grub-line rider naow he's inherited him a ranch what he never done nothin' fer to git?"

"Just the point, Ike," and Fay had smiled. When this bonny girl with the fair Scotch complexion and the firm little chin smiled, something happened to the hearts of old men and young alike. "Tedro's been a roving drifter and he never will settle down and tend to business—unless he has help."

"Sa-ay, what's yore interest in that jasper? I hearn tell he's a humdingin' rider an' roper an' can show off swelligant at a rodeo. You've seen 'im a-doin' it. That why you kinder—uh—fell fer 'im? . . . That crusty ol' bach'ler uncle o' hisn sent him tuh some highfalutin' school—'til he up and ran away from it. That was atter his own folks went over the Divide leavin' him nawthin' but his paw's name. I hearn—"

"And his father's thriftlessness, too, his utter lack of any sense of responsibility," said the girl. "I—well, I think there's something to him—if it's ever brought out. . . . Ike, I've already told Tedro I knew just the cowhand he needed—you."

And that settled it. Ike Bowlaigs, sixty if he was a day, but still as spry as a monkey, had gone to work for Tedro Ames.

However, on this particular morning eighteen months later, Fay McKenzie saw the veteran cowhand riding across the sagebrush flat directly toward the Half Moon Ranch, and a premonition of disaster clutched the girl's heart, for he led a horse packed with his bed and his war sack.

As Ike crossed the highway, which ran north and south following the wide valley of Swiftwater River, three collie dogs rushed vociferously to greet him. Always there had been collies on the Half Moon; venerable and shaggy oldsters, dogs in their prime very useful around the stock, and rollicky, playful puppies. No true Scotch outfit is complete otherwise.

These three were delighted to see an old acquaintance, and Ike, swinging off to open the gate, "woolled" them fondly for a few moments before he mounted, spat out his quid, wiped his lips and his saddle-colored mustache and reined up confronting the young woman awaiting him in the yard.

"Ye-eh, I quit," he blurted, fastening magpie-sharp eyes under bristling gray eyebrows upon her almost defiantly. "Don't you start a-bawlin' me out 'til you larn—Gosh all tomahawks an' a couple o' scalpin' knives, hain't nobody with hoss sense could stick an' work fer young Ames. Everybody in the hull county a-laughin' at him an' he hain't tumbled to it yet."

A spasm of pain crossed the girl's features. She knew this was true. But she said no word for Ike was getting his tongue unlimbered.

"Yere I takes care o' his cows, year ago las' summer,

14

a-herdin' 'em back in the high country and a-bringin' 'em home to him, come fall, and what's he done on the ranch while I been gone, hey? Nawthin'! Thirty head o' hosses he's got, but did that lazy jasper hire him a crew an' stack his hay? Nope. Contracted the job did fer half.

"Then what was we up again'? Buyin' feed fer winter, b'gosh. Did that set him back? You answer. Tedro hadn't done no irrigatin', hadn't patched his fences, ner buildin's. Things goin' all tuh hell. I feeds his cows through the winter. Me, who never forked hay fer no man afore. I takes his herd to the high range ag'in and rides close herd on 'em and I delivers 'em back to the T A ag'in this fall all hunkydory, three hundred and four head.

"What'd I find. Less hay'n ever an' half o' that not ourn, 'cause Tedro had again contracted the job. An' the fences—Gosh! Ain't no grass in his fields 'cause range stock et it up this fall. I has argered with that cub 'til I'm black in the face. No use! Now comes the last straw."

From his overalls pocket Ike Bowlaigs produced the *Swiftwater Star* which had lain on Tedro Ames' stove at dawn. "Look thar," pointing with a gnarled forefinger. "Frank Carter has stole a hundred cows and calves offen him. That'll 'gut' his herd. When I seen that I seen red. And look at this: 'Eleven hosses fer one!'"

Fay McKenzie read the second item with more interest than the first. She looked up at the scraggly veteran with a very strange light in her soft blue eyes,

15

and the paper rustled because her hand was trembling. She said: "Ike, Dad and the cowboys are trailing our beef herd to Harpoon. Until Foreman Jess gets home, you be your own boss. . . . Put your bed in the bunkhouse and find something to do."

"You mean I'm workin' fer the ol' Half Moon ag'in?"

"Of course."

"Ya-whoops!" Ike tossed his brindle hat in the air. "Sandy, you're shore a white man. Not one word a— a—reproachfullerin' me. . . . Honest I done the best I knowed, but Tedro—he's a likable cuss at that—he's throwin' 'er all tuh hell and—and, wal they was a little somethin' else, too.

"You'll laugh, but layin' on his table 's mornin' was a pink anterlope. I picked 'er up an' seen through it again' the light. Sandy, *I seen the ace of spades!"*

Fay's eyes widened. Range raised, she had known and associated with cowboys all her life; had known other rough and often very ignorant men. She therefore knew of their pet superstitions. Ike was going on:

"I wouldn't scare you fer nawthin', but the ace o' spades is *the death card,* and lookit that paper—the front page, Smith bushwhacked yesterday, the ace of spades was on his breast. Gosh all tomahawks, it's got me screwy a'ready."

"What nonsense," said the girl. But as she read the account of Paul Smith's death her face whitened.

Ike swallowed hard twice, then, noting her alarm said quickly: "Aw, it doan mean nawthin'. Nawthin'!

. . . Tedro'll likely be along soon with Apache. Maybe you can talk some sense into his empty haid. Reckon you still kinder like him."

"I still kind of like him—too much, but—" Fay broke off and turning ran quickly to the house. Ike, who was a wise old range hand, thought she was "a-goin' to have her a right good cry."

However, Ike was mistaken. Fay's eyes were dry and hot but tearless. As her father's secretary she attended to correspondence and did such bookkeeping as was necessary on the big Half Moon. She walked now to the small den, which was Bill McKenzie's office and hers. There was a fireplace, comfortable chairs, elk, deer and bear heads on the walls, a buffalo robe on the floor, two desks, a littered table, and in one corner a substantial steel safe.

From the table the girl selected one of several letters which had come in yesterday's mail:

"Dear Mr. McKenzie: I am writing to inquire if you would be willing to sign a promissory note in the sum of one thousand dollars for Mr. Tedro Ames?

"When I told Mr. Ames that our bank could not advance him this cash without the endorsement of some reliable stockman, like yourself, he said he thought you would be glad to accommodate him in this matter.

"Harmon H. Truesdale, President
"Stockmans' Bank of Swiftwater."

Fay stepped to the fireplace, touched a match to the letter and its envelope and watched flames consume them both.

"There. Dad'll never see that," she whispered. "Why, he'd lift the roof off the house. I can hear him snort: 'The nerve of some people! Go on a note for a fellow who's shown he can't run his dinky outfit? I should say not!' . . . And Dad doesn't know the half of it yet."

The girl heard Ike Bowlaigs in the living room paying his respects to Mrs. McKenzie, and she listened for a moment to the always delightful Scotch accent of her mother, who was whole-heartedly pleased to see the old cowpuncher.

"So ye're back once again, Ike. I'm sur-r-ly gla-ad to see you. But did ye leave Tedr-r-o without any help at all?"

Feeling that if she heard any further mention of young Tedro Ames she would go wild, Fay slipped outside by way of the kitchen. For a moment she stood gazing westward across the wide valley to the aloof and somber mountains, which seemed only a stone's throw distant.

Forested slopes and bald ridges vivid in the morning sunlight; shadows lingering in deep canyons, fog-mist hovering over the highest peaks—Flame Peaks, far to the north. A rough, high, defiant and unconquerable range, for, in one unbroken stretch forty miles long, no known trail led across these Flame Mountains.

However, the foothills and the valleys adjacent to the range—all small streams draining into Swiftwater River—was a land of thrifty ranchers, big and little, of hard-riding cowboys, of horses, cattle, wild game; a land where strife had been known, the early cowmen's war against the settlers, which the big cowmen had lost; the fight to hold the range for cattle against the invasion of sheep which had been won, and the never-ending war against night riding rustlers, horse thieves and even out-and-out outlaws.

However, Fay McKenzie, known as Sandy, was not thinking of outlaws this morning. Oh, no. Her thoughts were of one, Tedro Ames, and thoughts of this happy-go-lucky fellow brought other suitors to her mind. Chief among these was Leonard M. Stoddard, thrifty, shrewd, far-sighted, ambitious. Hard work and singleness of purpose had left its stamp upon him and perhaps robbed him of that something all young men should have, gaiety, love of fun, that rollicking sense of humor, the joys of cameraderie and of being a good fellow.

Very serious was Len Stoddard. But folks spoke of him most respectfully as "a comer," "a go-getter," "a worker." He and his brother Jake had come to Swiftwater Valley with a wagon and team, three saddle horses and a small herd of cows five years ago. They had filed on homesteads and desert claims and had prospered amazingly.

"Thrift, hard work and strict tending to business," old Bill McKenzie said approvingly. And when

Leonard came courting Fay, old Bill offered no objection.

On the other hand Tedro Ames had never met with McKenzie's approval. "No gumption, no initiative. Easy come, easy go and t'hell with tomorrow." Yet old Bill had been very tolerant because, like all the other old timers, he simply couldn't help liking Tedro Ames.

Now on this lovely fall morning Fay McKenzie was comparing Len Stoddard with Tedro Ames and Tedro suffered much by the comparison.

Lost in her unhappy musing she suddenly became aware of the rattle of wheels and the squeak and rustle of harness leather. Looking up she saw Hank Farnum's stagecoach swinging along the road southward bound for Harpoon on the railroad. The black-hatted, black-mustached spry and wizened old stage driver was a very familiar figure. Every day, except Sundays, for nine years now, he had driven past the Half Moon ranch. At Goose Creek Canyon he met the other driver coming from Harpoon. They exchanged loads, ate dinner, changed horses and turned back, Hank returning to Swiftwater, the other man to Harpoon.

Ranchers fortunate enough to live along the main highway had rural delivery. So Fay now ran out to meet the stage, and Hank's faded gray eyes and the ridges of his weathered face beamed as always at sight of the winsome girl.

" 'Lo, there, Sandy," familiarly. "Lookin' pert as a

20

young colt this mornin'. I got that spool o' thread and the other gee-gaws fer yore ma. Here they be and here's yore mail sack. . . . Get up, nags."

Fay of course was smiling. Bright-eyed once again. She thanked the driver, then called: "Wait a minute, Hank. What's the sheriff found out about who shot Paul Smith?"

"Prezactly nothin'," said Hank, disgustedly. " 'Course the fat-head we got for a sheriff wouldn't. . . . Sorenson, his neighbor, a kinder suspect, had him a airtight alibi. Smith was shot with a .45-.70 Winchester. 'Parently the killer left no sign a-tall."

The stage squeaked and rattled onward. Fay opened the mail sack, sorted the letters. What was this? A square, pink envelope, the address typewritten; no return address; the postmark "Swiftwater, Colorado".

For some reason the girl's hands were shaking as she took from the envelope a playing card and nothing else. The card was an ace of spades!

CHAPTER TWO
ONE SHOT FROM THE BRUSH

Tedro Ames would have slept until noon, such had become his habit of late, had not grizzled old Frank Carter come stamping into the T A house before the sun was an hour high. Carter, leathery of face, aggressive and loud-spoken, kicked open Tedro's door, dragged the bed covers from the young rancher's bunk, dumped them on the floor and bellowed:

"Snap outa it! I come to get them cows. Straddle yore cayuse an' give us a hand."

"Brought help with you to drive 'em home, didn't you?" Tedro countered. "Round up the field and cut out the cows yourself. . . . Ike'll help you."

"He ain't 'round no place, Tedro. Writ on a pink envelope on yore table is: 'I've quit. Send me my wages. Ike.'"

"Uh? The heck you say." Tedro blinked, rubbed his eyes and reached for his trousers. "So that old long-horn has up and quit me at last. He's threatened to time and again."

"And no wonder," snorted Frank Carter. "Tedro, you used to punch cows fer me and I fired you three-four times, but always give you 'nother chance. Why did I? 'Cause you savvy horses and cows and 'd be a plumb good hand if you'd 'tend to business. But, aw, hell, you got no sense o' responsibility. . . . 'Course I brung help with me to get the dogies. Noisy, Bug and Slim Shafter's out there on their hosses. They had seen the paper and all the way down from the ranch to here they was laughin' fit to bust 'emselves. Laughin' at you. Snorty Cow, if this keeps up all the cowboys'll hooraw you every time you show yore face."

Tedro grunted twice, grinned and replied: "S'pose the boys was laughin' 'cause Frank R. Carter slickered me in a deal. But you didn't gyp me so bad, Frank, because there's only a hundred and two cows with calves. So you got just two cut backs. Ha-hoo!"

His chuckle was instantly hushed as Carter retorted: "I knowed that when I bought 'em. I'd been out here, givin' the T A herd the once over. But as usual you wasn't home. Don't you never stay home, never work?"

"None of your business." Tedro Ames was flushing for some reason. "You paid the money to the bank as agreed?"

"Uh-huh. You won't get a nickel outa this sale for yourself. Harmon Truesdale said he wished now he had included your hosses in the mortgage as well as ranch and cattle. That might ha' kept you from swappin' 'leven picked broncs fer one pinto pony. That's what the waddies was chortlin' most about. Of all the fool—"

"Get out, before I heave a boot at you!" Tedro's mild brown eyes were flashing dangerously. "Lots of busybodies in this neck of the woods. You're one!"

Carter went abruptly out and Tedro Ames heard his cowpunchers laughing as they loped away. A minute later the young ranchman walked to his outer door, stood for a minute gazing southward across the dense willows along the stream which ran behind his tumble-down shed and tumble-down corrals. In the meadow beyond the willows Carter and his waddies were whooping the T A cattle into one bunch. Hoof-beats sounded from the north and a horseman rode around the log cabin into Tedro's line of vision. A stoop-shouldered, gangling individual with greasy overalls, greasy jumper, greasy cap pulled over his

23

ears and a greasy face, he was Roy Holderness, nick-named Greasy of course.

"Hi thar, Tedro. You up a'ready? I come to get them hosses. Ike ain't got 'em corralled?"

"Corral 'em yourself. You'll find the whole bunch in the pasture."

"Heh-heh," cackled Holderness. "You must have a hangover, you act so daggoned testy. Or what opsott you? I was a-tellin' some of the boys how Tedro Ames shore knowed what he was about an' got what he went after."

Was this sarcasm? It was, for Greasy was winking at nothing in particular. Tedro could not recall a day which had started off quite so badly.

"Fust hoss I'm pickin' is the saddler you was forkin' yest'day," the man announced.

"Take him and ten more," shortly. "Leave the rest in the corral. S'pose I'll have to bust a green bronc or ride an old crowbait."

"Heh-heh! The jaunty Tedro Ames ridin' a stove-up ol' crowbait tuh see his gal and take her the pinto. But he'll ferget what he's ridin' when she smiles. Heh-heh!" Grinning toothlessly Holderness flicked his mount with a willow switch and loped to wrangle the cavvy.

Tedro was riding a long-toothed and spavined old "crowbait" that had once been pensioned, when, three hours later, he led Apache into the yard at the Half Moon ranch. However, the young man himself was clean shaven; wore a clean white shirt and a fancy

24

blue necktie and his snow-white Beaver Stetson sat at a jaunty angle. He loved fine clothes. Even before he'd become a rancher he had "put his wages on his back" as they say on the range. But the pinto, curried and brushed even to its flowing mane and tail, outshone Tedro. It looked like a million dollars.

Three dogs, Ned, Scotty and Collie, barking joyfully, rushed to greet the new arrival, though strangely no one else appeared. Tedro rode up in front of the neat, roomy log house—such a house as he'd have some day—and called: "Sandy! Yoho, Sandy!"

To his immense relief the girl came out and stood on the porch with sunlight flooding her tawny hair. Slender, willowy, wearing a sort of creamy-white dress, loose about her shapely throat, Tedro knew she was the prettiest lady in all the world and most adorable.

But what was wrong? Why didn't her bright eyes light with pleasure? Never had she seemed so frigid and utterly unattainable.

"Good morning, Tedro." No warmth, no gladness in her greeting, and Tedro Ames, usually able to hold up his end in any conversation, was for the moment speechless.

"Never saw you ride such a sorry-looking nag, Tedro. Thought your Uncle Jeff pensioned old Shaggy years ago?"

"Uh?" Tedro Ames hated himself for grunting, but just couldn't help it. "Uh-uh?" He felt his face flaming red and ever redder. "But don't you see *Apache?*" he blurted. "I've brought you the pinto. He's a present for the sweetest—"

"No," said the girl. "I never gave you reason to suppose I could accept such a present as a horse from you. And now—"

"Fay, you ain't actin' like yourself. Don't you remember telling me how bad you wanted this pinto hoss?" Tedro felt more and more dismayed and bewildered. The inconsistencies of the feminine mind were dark mysteries to him.

"And now," Fay rushed on, her voice high and unnatural, "I couldn't, wouldn't accept Apache even though we were engaged. Which we are not *and never will be.* Oh, Tedro, don't you, can't you see where you're drifting? How you've made yourself the laughing stock of the whole county? Those items in the *Swiftwater Star.* Editor Thomas hoorawing you, proclaiming to the world that you were—are—a fool.

"Did you ever consider how humiliating such silly things as you do, such items as those last and others that popped out earlier, are to me? Don't you realize that you're throwing away the outfit your uncle left you? That you—well as Dad or Ike or any old cowman would say—you don't amount to two whoops. Tedro, take a tumble to yourself. . . . Goodbye."

As though this were a bad dream, Tedro Ames saw the girl turn and pass through the door which closed behind her with a click which seemed to shut him out of her life, even as she vanished from his sight. How could he know that her heart was breaking? That with handkerchief pressed to her eyes she stumbled blindly to her own room where she buried her hot face in a pillow soon to be dampened with tears.

But Tedro did not know this. For a long minute he sat bolt upright in his saddle as though made of stone. Then, as though still in a dream, he turned the sorry nag, once pensioned, and rode slowly away. Shaggy would have headed straight across the sage for home, but with a fierce cut of spurs and tug at the bridle Tedro turned the venerable horse along the road leading to Swiftwater.

As he rode, to his bewildered mind came a certain defiance mingled with a reckless I'll show the world attitude. Women? He was through with 'em! She'd said he was a fool, the laughing stock of the county, that Ray Thomas was hoorawing him in the *Swiftwater Star*. But not yet was he willing to admit that Fay McKenzie had been right. The nosey gossips who knew everything about a fellow's business and never minded their own were the fools.

"I'll show 'em all, Sandy, too," Tedro proclaimed to the pinto horse which led up alongside old Shaggy. "I'll make 'em laugh outa the other side of their mouths." Then irrelevantly: "You damn pinto nag, I hate you. Hate you! She said she wanted you, the worst way. I swap for you, she throws me down. I'll—"

He had reached no plan of action when he crossed Brush Creek which flowed into Swiftwater River from

27

the high divide to eastward. As he rode out of the heavy willows on the farther side of this a mounted man materialized as though magically in front of him. Tedro had never before seen the fellow, scarcely saw him now and would have ridden right on without a word had not the other lifted a slender, dark hand and spoken:

"Right nifty pony you're leadin', stranger."

"Uh-huh," shortly and sourly.

"I'm forkin' a tolerable good bronc myself, but I might talk trade with you."

Tedro pulled up most abruptly. Trade? This jasper wanted to talk trade! Tedro had been about to turn Apache loose, for he would not lead the horse into town and have all the boys hoorawin' him. They'd guy him to death. In fancy he could hear the tongues going clack, clack. But here was a Heaven-sent chance to get rid of the accursed pinto that had cost him eleven good horses—a cool thousand dollars worth of horses and had lost him his sweetheart.

"Huh? I don't call that stockin'-legged bay no hoss a-tall, Mister," he snorted. "Howsoever, if you'd mention boot and plenty of it—" Fifty or a hundred dollars would come in mighty handy to a fellow who was busted. Not a red cent realized from the sale of a hundred cows and calves; bills overdue at all the stores — and saloons too.

The stranger, he was tall, lean and very swarthy with a jutting chin, hook-nose, high cheekbones and the blackest of eyes, shrugged and said with surprising candor for any horse trader: "When I get stuck on a hoss, I don't arger and beat 'round the bush. 'Fact I'm knowed as 'Quick Trader Markley!' "

He produced a bill of sale for the stocking-legged bay and handed it to Tedro who said: "This looks jake. Glad to know you, Markley. I got a bill of sale to this pinto race hoss, too. Here 'tis. Now how 'bout a hundred bucks t' boot?"

Tedro got a hundred dollars boot. He changed his saddle to his new mount while the other man placed his rig on the pinto, said, "Glad to have met you" and rode into the willows.

Turning Shaggy loose to find his way home, Tedro rode on to Swiftwater, feeling one hundred per cent better. Cash in his pocket, a good hoss between his knees. Of course the brand on the bay was so blotched he couldn't read it, and he hadn't known Markley. But— Aw, the deal was O.K. He had a bill of sale.

After stabling his new mount he sauntered up town with his usual sang-froid, hat pushed back, spurs a-jingle, jaunty, carefree. No one could have told of the tumult under that curly black hair. But the bartender of the Ever Open Saloon detected a strange gleam in Tedro's usually mild brown eyes and never had this bartender seen the young rancher consume so many straight whiskies.

Tedro Ames was soon buying for the house; was soon gloriously drunk and singing. This went on all afternoon. Yet toward dusk, when he saw Leonard M.

Stoddard come in, he was sober enough to glare at this lanky, rock-faced man. Somewhere in the back of Tedro's mind was a twinge of jealous rage. Stoddard would now be riding top horse with the daughter of the Half Moon. Aw heck, it didn't matter—didn't matter. Nothin' mattered. Stoddard's brother, Jake, was with him, stockier and more powerfully built than Leonard, quiet, emotionless, cold-eyed; also the man they called their foreman, a comparative newcomer, Ab Thurston, plainly a real cowman.

"Step up, boys," whooped Tedro. "I'm treatin'. Ya-ho-hic, happiest daggoned jasper as ever forked a buckin' hoss. What'll it be, fellers? Tedro Ames buyin'."

"Celebratin' your puttin' one over on me?" Len Stoddard asked casually.

"Uh? Oh, that pinto hoss. You wanted Apache pretty bad, Len?"

"I admit it. Where's the hoss now?"

"Where's the pinto now?" Young Ames roared with laughter. "Where you think Apache is now? Give you three guesses, Len. That darned Thomas said in his paper, 'dirt cheap at any price.' He was more'n correct. Stoddard, you shouldn't ought to ha' been so tight. Pay the price asked, that's what I sez. Ya-whoops. Fill 'em up, barkeep. You been water-foundered or are you jus' naturally so daggoned slow?"

Leonard Stoddard drew Jake aside whispering to him, but Tedro's ears were keen. He caught, "The cheerful idiot has give Fay the hoss. He's standin' ace high with her now o' course."

"'Course," muttered Jake, "and celebratin' by gettin' drunker'n seven hundred dollars."

Len fastened a flinty and challenging eye on young Ames: "I've heard you was some poker player. Game to match your skill agin mine?"

"Unlucky in love, lucky at cards," quoted Tedro, grinning tantalizingly at the aggressive Stoddard. But his private thought ran: If that old superstition's true I ought to win, though Len don't yet know I'm the unlucky lover. Aloud he called: "Bartender, a new deck, and watch me take those Stoddards to a cleanin'."

"If you're short o' cards," called one rancher, "I got an ace of spades what some fool sent me in a pink envelope."

Sudden silence, those in the saloon looking askance at each other.

"What them black aces mean?" demanded Tedro, sliding into a chair at a green-topped table and hauling out his money, bills and silver. "I got one, too."

"I've heard they mean death," said the bartender in a hushed voice. "Death!"

"Bunk!" snorted Tedro. "Cut fer deal, Len? Jus' you an' me an' Jake a-playin'?"

"I wouldn't snort," spoke Boyd Loomis, the handsome merchant. "'Member, boys, Paul Smith was shot in the back and an ace of spades was on his breast bone. Yep, they mean death. There's—"

"Here's to death!" Tedro jeered recklessly and lifted a quart bottle of whisky to his lips.

"—some sinister and awful threat hoverin' over this range," Loomis went on. "I've seen five ranchers and one man in town who've had pink envelopes—"

"Pink snakes," chuckled Tedro Ames. "Yore deal, Len. Bettin' you five bucks afore I look at my cards."

Thus began the never-to-be-forgotten poker game in the Ever Open Saloon. Ab Thurston sat in a chair at the same table, taking no part. Every other man in the room crowded close around the gamblers, and Tedro, defiant and reckless, played with a wild abandon. He won five hundred dollars from the brothers, bet the wad against a like amount and lost.

He offered to put up his remaining horses and lost them—all except the bay for which he had recently traded and about which he said nothing. He lost his saddle, his gun, his chaps, his spurs, his fine beaver Stetson and still he would not quit.

"Gimme a chance to get back at you, Len," he demanded. "I'm the kind of a jasper who lets the tail go with the hide. My equity in the T A ranch and the cattle on it against three thousand bucks. What say?"

Leonard M. Stoddard, without the slightest change of expression, wrote a check for three thousand dollars and laid it on the table.

"That good?" demanded Tedro with sudden caution. "You actually got that much jack in the bank?"

"Harmon Truesdale is here," said Stoddard. "Hi, Mr. Truesdale, how about my check?"

The president of the bank said the check was as good as gold.

"Then let 'er rip," whooped Tedro Ames joyfully. He'd win, he knew, for that old axiom must have some truth back of it, "Unlucky in love; lucky at cards."

He peeped at four aces and a deuce in his hand, said "I'll play these," and vaguely noticed the ring of tense silent faces in the smoke-hazy yellow lamplight; felt the silence where men scarcely breathed. Jake Stoddard was no longer in the game. Len said quietly, "I draw one." Then he laid down his cards face up—a straight flush in spades, king high, stared at Tedro. He spread out his four aces, ran a hand through his curly hair and rose slowly to his feet. "No argument, but that silly axiom shore ain't true. T' hell with all superstitions anyhow," he heard himself say, and abruptly the room came out of its strange silent tension. Some one gasped, "Whee!" Then: "Ain't he a dead game loser!"

Tedro reached the bar, rallied and laughed, his old reckless devil-may-care laugh: "No hard feelings, Stoddards. None. I'm right where I was afore I got the T A. Busted and in debt. And what of it?"

The swinging doors parted with a violent swish and the sheriff of Swiftwater charged into the big room, with his gun in his hand. He was a young man, blond, fleshy, moon-faced with rolls of fat under his small eyes. He stopped and threw a searching glance about, expelled his breath and asked:

"There ain't nobody else here? Nobody went out the back door?"

"No," said the bartender. "What—?"

"Boys," Sheriff Potter spoke in a tense whisper, "I'm a-lookin' fer that darned bandit, Wolf Whalen. I sighted him t'day out on the range, but he disappeared too suddent for me tuh get 'im. He rides a stockin'-legged bay hoss knowed to all us officers."

Silence for a moment then some one began: "You think he'd dare come to town?"

"Like as not," growled the sheriff. "Plumb nervy that outlaw. Would I like to collect the thousand bucks on his scalp!"

Tedro Ames considered the label on a whisky bottle without really seeing it at all. A stocking-legged bay horse? "Potter, what's Wolf Whalen look like?" he asked.

"Tall, swart, with a hook nose, black, black eyes, dinky black mustache, and he's lean, tough, wiry," the sheriff replied. "Why you ask?"

"No reason a-tall," drawled Tedro indifferently, but a dry smile played on his lips. "Len, if you'll loan me the use of what was my saddle I'll be goin' out to the T A, pickin' up a few duds and ridin' on. On and on and on, don't give a damn where."

"Sure," Stoddard returned. "Ab," to his silent foreman, "go with Tedro. Take charge of the T A ranch. I'll be over to see you in the mornin'."

Bareheaded, gunless, spurless, but with a quart bottle, Tedro accompanied the two Stoddards to the stable. In the dim light no one seemed to notice that Tedro's mount was a stocking-legged bay. But when they had saddled, Leonard recalled that he was carrying Tedro's white Stetson.

"Here, Ab, I'll make you a present," he said, and plucking Ab Thurston's' old black hat from that individual's head he placed the white one on it.

"Tedro, a bonnet for you," and Tedro accepted the old black sombrero. He and the quiet fellow, Ab Thurston, arrived in due course at the dark, silent T A ranch. Tedro no longer singing or even talking was drowsy and stupid, his mind numb. Mechanically he slid from his saddle in front of the tumbledown shed.

"Hay 'nuff for your hoss in there, Ab. I'll be ridin' on t'night."

"Get you some shut-eye," returned the tall fellow gruffly. "You need it. Put a good feed under your belt in the mornin' afore you go. Besides, I got somethin' to tell you—when you're sober enough to know sic-'em."

"Uk-unn. Ridin' on now. Laughin' stock of the whole county, me. Plain damn fool, me. Nobody cares two whoops in a wash tub. All the punchers'll hooraw me worse'n ever. Couldn't work for nobody in this neck-the-woods. Headin' fer a new range, Ab, t'night. Hey! Don't you lead my hoss in there. My hoss? Outlaw Wolf Whalen's hoss. That's a good un.

"Leadin' 'im in anyhow? . . . Well, Ab, go on to the shanty, an' light up. Me, I want to see if I can think."

Tedro rested his head in his hands leaning against the corral. He was aware after what seemed some time that lamplight sprang up in the cabin across the yard, and from one eye he saw Ab Thurston's figure in the light at the door of the cabin. The white, white Stetson—Tedro's hat—pulled low on the man's head, seemed to loom up like a white steer in a red herd.

Abruptly something happened to the man, Ab Thurston. He threw his arms wide in a frantic gesture, pitched forward and collapsed on the gravel just outside the door. In Tedro's ears rang the sharp, decisive crack of a rifle. He pinched himself, rubbed his tired eyes. This must be a nightmare. Yet, yonder in the shaft of light Thurston's body was very still—as still as the night.

Forgetting that he had no gun the cowboy galvanized to action and rushed to the nearby willows from which the shot had sounded. Silence and darkness there mocked him. Search, he realized, was utterly futile. On winged feet he crossed the yard to the cabin and bent to look closely at the prone figure. The bullet from the dark had struck Thurston between his eyes, and Tedro's white beaver Stetson, still on the man's head, was now crimsoned with blood.

CHAPTER THREE
TWENTY THOUSAND DOLLARS THE PRICE

William Tecumseh Sherman Johnsing Brown, the darky cook of the Half Moon ranch, regulated his kitchen clock by Hank Farnum's stage. At eight every morning except Sundays, Hank's four bay horses drawing his venerable Concord Coach came racing around a bend of the road, swung into the straightway leading past the Half Moon and stopped for a moment at the mail box just outside the gate.

W.T.S. Johnsing Brown, known to all Half Moon cowpunchers and others as Tecumseh, looked at his clock on this particular morning and decided it must be five minutes fast. Out yonder on the road Hank Farnum had just arrived. But li'le Miz Sandy McKenzie had been waiting at the mail box for fully fifteen minutes. Sump'n bawtherin' her, Tecumseh could tell.

Miz Sandy wasn't so happy like she had been yest'day mawnin' 'fore Ike Bowlaigs rid in. She hadn't been a bit glad to see Tedro Ames, hadn't taken the fine hawse, Apache, from him neither. An' Tedro had rid away lookin' like a feller who'd los' his best friend. That jolly feller what a nigger jus' couldn't help likin' heaps had did somethin' to make Miz Sandy unhappy. This mawnin' she had been up terrible early, out for a ride 'fore breakfast and then scannin' the road for the stage long 'fore it came.

She was greeting old Hank now and taking the ranch mail sack from him, and Hank, though time was precious to him, was lingerin' an' talkin'. Tecumseh wished he could hear what they were saying. He couldn't, but Hank Farnum was answering a question which Fay had tried hard not to have seemed too eager.

"Was Tedro in town las' night? He was thar with bells on. 'Fact he run plumb—" abruptly Hank coughed discreetly behind his heavy mustache. "She's a sweet mornin' for September, ain't she?"

"Yes. Fall's always pretty, Hank. Tedro run plumb—?"

"Hawg wild, if you must know, Sandy. You'd larn it from somebody else anyhow. He never got down but he shore was lookin' on the likker when she was red, and, I seen it my own self—the daggondest, rip-tootin' poker game."

"Oh," said Fay in a small voice. "Oh." But she thought: "So that's the way he took it. Got gloriously drunk and gambled instead of—instead of what? What exactly did you expect he'd do, Fay McKenzie? . . . I think you hoped he'd go home and strip off his showy duds, get into a pair of dirty overalls and go to work."

"You'll soon larn this, too, li'le girl," Hank was saying. "Tedro lost every dad-blamed thing he had left, his hat even, his spurs, his gun and his ranch to them Stoddard Brothers."

"Hank, is that the truth?"

The driver nodded vigorously. "Ain't no other news much. Sheriff Potter ain't found no clue as to who bushwhacked Paul Smith. But, say, them pink envelopes, in each an ace of spades, nawthin' else, has shore got folks wonderin'; got some scairt, too. You heard 'bout 'em?"

"Yes," said Fay. "What's Tedro Ames going to do now?"

Hank hunched his shoulders. "Search me. Reckon I'd better shack along. Ged-up, Kate, Sunny."

Fay stood gazing after the stage and not seeing it at all. She whispered to the bright morning: "I wonder if Len Stoddard won Apache as well as everything else Tedro owned. . . . If Stoddard thinks he can give me that horse he's much mistaken. Oh, Tedro, why'd you do it?"

She opened the mail sack and stood as though transfixed staring at one particular envelope—a square pink envelope. After a moment Fay picked this up, somewhat as if it were an obnoxious bug, and turned it over. The postmark this time was Harpoon, Colorado. The typewritten address: "Miss Fay McKenzie, Swiftwater, Colorado."

"So the Black Aces are honoring me now," she said and took from the envelope an ace of spades. Written with pen and ink on the card was a message:

"Fay McKenzie: Put twenty thousand dollars, unmarked bills or gold coin, at the base of the lone pine on Wind Ridge at twilight tomorrow

39

night, Saturday night. Come alone to the spot, unarmed. Leave the money and go home immediately.

"Fail to obey and your father will *not* reach home from shipping cattle *alive*. Black Aces."

Every vestige of color drained from the girl's pretty face. Except for a few winters away at school, she had lived all her life on the range and although she had read of extortion plots had never dreamed of anything such as this confronting her. "Black Aces" the threat was signed and a spade ace had been found on the breast of murdered Paul Smith!

She rallied after a moment, thinking, thinking. She must keep this vile threat from her mother. Mrs. McKenzie wasn't in the best of health these days and a terrific shock would send her to bed, might even cause her death. To whom could Fay go for advice and help? If her father were at home she could imagine his wrathful explosion; his stubborn and final refusal to accede to any such demand.

The foreman, Jess Walker, and the cowboys might reach the ranch from Harpoon tonight. But what could they do? Nothing to save Bill McKenzie's life when Bill was riding the stock train to market. Obviously these Black Aces, whoever they were, would have some assassin posted to murder McKenzie—if their demand was not complied with.

Fay thought of talking with the two ranch hands and the blacksmith, the only help now on the Half Moon, but concluded they could offer no advice that would help her with this thorny problem. As for Ike Bowlaigs—he was a pretty wise "old head"—but his one idea of fighting anything was to go after it with a smoking gun and how could you fight some intangible menace that worked in the dark, unseen, with a gun? Besides, Ike had left the ranch immediately after breakfast to ride in the rough hills looking for odd cattle the roundup might have missed. He would not likely return till night.

The troubled girl thought of Tedro, and she shook her sorrel curls. She had put him out of her life—if not out of her thoughts—and she could not go asking him for any favors. Of what use anyhow? Tedro had never yet shown any ability as a thinker, strategist, fighter.

She hid the hateful pink envelope in her dress, glanced at the rest of the mail and composing her features walked to the house. Tecumseh met her at the door: "Lawsy, Miz Sandy, sump'n done give yo a most awful turn. Wha's—?"

"Just your imagination," the girl countered steadily, while thinking: "Good Heavens, if Tecumseh was to get his white eyes on one of those black aces we'd be short a cook and a good one. Not even the rabbit's foot in his hip pocket would hold him."

Brushing past the negro she handed the mail to her mother in the living room and remarked nonchalantly: "I think I'll lope in to Swiftwater, mumsy."

No need of explaining why and Mrs. McKenzie

asked for no reason. But if twenty thousand must be raised, banker Harmon Truesdale must be consulted. The small safe in the Half Moon office held only a few hundred dollars at any time and the Half Moon checking account contained less than four thousand dollars.

"I'll have to borrow money, and how'll I ever explain to Daddy," thought Fay as she changed to her riding togs, overalls, serviceable boots, a man's shirt and short leather jacket, a nutria Stetson that matched well her tawny hair.

So poised, so outwardly composed was the girl of the Half Moon that her mother failed to notice anything out of the ordinary when Fay kissed the older woman good-bye and went out to the stable. But something blurred her vision and her hands were very shaky as she saddled a blood-bay pony named Torchy. Once out on the road she spurred fast, lips compressed, eyes looking straight ahead and with her rode worry, such a worry as she had never before known.

Swiftwater's log and frame houses sat on a sagebrush hill above the valley of Swiftwater River and to the east of it. Along its single main street, wide, dusty and the color of a faded yellow shirt, were numerous hitch rails but no lamp posts. However the false fronts of stores and saloons showed fresh paint as did also the substantial-looking bank and the hotel. For this was a prosperous little cow town. The prosperous ranchers made it so.

Today there was an undercurrent of excitement in the very air and as Fay swung down at a hitch rail, tying Torchy, she heard a tousled ragamuffin bawling an extra of the *Swiftwater Star.* The lad was new to this sort of thing but he was doing his "leather-lunged" best.

"RAY THOMAS VISITED BY MASKED MAN AND TIED UP. ORDERED TO PRINT BLACK ACES ANNOUNCEMENT. READ ALL 'BOUT IT!"

"What's this?" cried the girl breathlessly. "An extra of the *Star.* I never heard of Thomas getting out—"

"Here you are, Miz Sandy," and the boy thrust a damp paper at her. "Two-bits, please. But it's wuth it, doan you think?"

Fay parted with a quarter and read for herself the black headline, followed by:

"Ye Editor's home invaded by masked des-perado! Shortly after midnight while lights were out and the town slept. More correctly while lights still glowed in the Ever Open Saloon and a curious crowd watched Tedro Ames gamble away the last vestige of his inheritance. . . ."

Fay winced. Would Ray Thomas never cease hoorawing poor Tedro? She wished he had had enough delicacy to leave this "dig" out of his sheet.

Her eyes picked up the thread of the editor's front-page story farther along.

"—he came with a cat-like tread, the masked desperado. Ye editor sat erect in his bed to find a lamp lighted in his room, an intruder menacing him with a six-shooter. (No foolin', boys, the muzzle of that gun looked like a cannon and the man's wicked eyes, gleaming yellow through the slits of his mask, gave me the creeps.)

"Spoke the intruder, 'I'm tyin' you hand and foot and gaggin' you so you won't yell ner foller me.' And he did just that. Then, placing on ye editor's dresser a black ace of spades, he snarled: 'You're to print in your paper what I tell you, this:

"'THE BLACK ACES ARE MORE THAN STRONG ENOUGH TO ENFORCE THEIR DEMANDS AND UTTERLY RUTHLESS. TAKE HEED ALL RANCHERS AND OTHERS WHO HAVE RECEIVED AND WHO WILL YET RECEIVE OUR INTRODUCTORY CARD. OBEY TO THE LETTER OUR ORDERS WHICH YOU WILL GET IN DUE COURSE, OR SUFFER, AS RANCHMAN PAUL SMITH HAS ALREADY SUFFERED, THE CONSEQUENCES OF HIS OWN RASH-NESS. OBEY AND BE SAFE. FAIL TO OBEY AND DIE!'

"We might remark in passing that the cowardly renegade seemed to have learned this piece by rote. We are printing this declaration because we think the citizens should know, not because of any dire threat against our person or property.

"Fellow citizens, arise. What is this menace which hovers over our fair community? Are we—?"

At this point, several townsmen joined the girl; Boyd Loomis, the hardware man, remarking lightly: "Gee whillikers, Thomas shore spread hisself. Look down there. He calls these Black Aces vermin and villains, yella-bellied cowards and nefarious extortionists all in one sentence. Sounds kinder silly to me, 'cause I just figger some drunk cowpunchers was playing a prank on him. . . . What's matter, Miz McKenzie? You look kinder—kinder bothered."

"Bothered? Not at all, not at all," said the girl. But there was a queer catch in her voice and a second citizen scowled at Loomis saying:

"You're the only jasper I've seen who thinks this business is silly or a joke. . . . The hull town's hopped-up, Miss Fay. Trade's at a standstill and folks are gathered in little bunches talking things over, mystified, wonderin' and scared—scared."

Fay excused herself and walked to the bank building. To the right, as she entered, was Harmon H. Truesdale's private office and through a half-opened door she saw Henry Kline, of the H K, connected, on

45

Burnt Fork Creek, closeted with the bank president. Truesdale was the principal stockholder of this thriving little bank, and although he hired a cashier-bookkeeper he personally attended to all business of importance.

Pausing inside the main room and sizing up the man, Fay felt, as she had always felt, his power. Something magnetic and dynamic about him. This was in his manner, his dignified bearing, his stature, for Truesdale was a big man physically as well as mentally. Iron-grey hair, bushy gray eyebrows and a closely trimmed gray mustache lent dignity to his broad face, a face always set in rather severe lines and always imperturbable.

Quite naturally this strong man was mayor of Swiftwater and regarded as its foremost citizen. Therefore Fay felt diffident, a bit awed, as she waited for the great man to finish his interview with Henry Kline.

Old Henry Kline, bachelor cowman, bewhiskered, bald and bow-legged, had dressed up for his visit to town by tying a red bandana around his corded throat and by putting on his coat which looked as if a tramp had grown tired of carrying it over his shoulder. Yet this slouchy, unkempt old settler, who chewed tobacco and never was known to wear a new hat, held a warm, warm place in Fay McKenzie's loyal little heart.

Waiting, the girl heard Truesdale's big fingers drum on his desk and then she caught her breath sharply as she heard the banker's deep, resonant voice: "Ten thousand dollars is a lot of money, Mr. Kline. Still your land and cattle are undoubtedly worth a good deal more—even at a forced sale. So, hum, if you insist, I'll see what I can do."

"Insist?" rumbled Kline. "You know darn well I never plastered nothin' o' mine fer a red cent afore, but this double-blanked card says— You read it."

Fay leaned forward peering into the room. The rancher had handed Truesdale an ace of spades. The banker read:

"Kline, put ten thousand dollars, cash, in the salt trough on hill north of your buildings before eight o'clock tonight, Friday night. Fail to do this or make any attempt to trap our messenger and you will be shot! Black Aces."

Again Truesdale drummed on his desk. Henry Kline blurted: "And by thunder, Paul Smith was shot! . . . Me, I can fight anything as comes in the open, but this— I better do 'er, hadn't I, banker?"

"I can't take the responsibility of advising you," Truesdale countered. "Possibly the sheriff might set a trap—"

"That bone-headed Pete Potter set a trap?" Kline's voice showed his scorn for the sheriff's ability. "Hell! If he did, I'd be shot anyhow. . . . Lend me the jack, Truesdale. Later, I'll get that damn coyote or coyote pack!"

"Let me amend that," said Truesdale grimly. "*We'll* get the coyote pack!" Calling his cashier he directed the young man to make out a mortgage and a note for Henry Kline, and to advance the cowman ten thousand dollars in cash. Whereupon Kline and the cashier stepped into a rear office.

A minute later Fay, her heart pounding though she tried to still it, was showing Truesdale her ace of spades, telling him of her fear for her father's life. "What'll I do?"

The great man of Swiftwater made a rather oracular reply: "It seems, Miss McKenzie, as if these extortionists have just opened their campaign. You saw the extra?" Fay nodded and he went on, "Obviously they intend to demand money, or something else, from many of us. Therefore they will be working in our midst until they collect from each individual threatened.

"This will give us time to act. They'll make a false step sooner or later and we'll capture them, recover such money as we are forced to give them, and publicly hang them, by George."

He turned in his swivel chair and drummed on his desk as if to indicate that the interview was over.

"You got to catch a calf before you can brand it," said Fay. "At present no one has any remote idea of who these thieves may be, and I need sixteen thousand dollars over and above the Half Moon checking account, which I can draw."

Truesdale faced her again: "You wish to sign a note

for that amount with the understanding that Bill McKenzie will stand back of it and pay the note? You own no interest in the Half Moon in your own right, do you?"

"I own my clothes, a cowboy outfit and three saddle horses," said Fay.

"Then we would have no legal obligation upon Mr. McKenzie to meet his daughter's obligation," said the banker very thoughtfully. "Mind, I'm dreadfully concerned, but no bank can lend money without ample security. . . . You might wire your father explaining the—"

The girl made an impatient gesture, smiled a tight-lipped little smile: "I know what he'd answer, six words, 'Tell them to go to hell!'"

"Knowing Bill McKenzie as I do, I think you're quite right," Truesdale agreed.

Fay cried a bit wildly: "I must have the money, for I can't bear the thought of Daddy's being shot."

The banker regarded her silently while she tried to read his eyes, his face, and failed. Suddenly he burst out: "I can't either! So, Miss McKenzie, I'll let you have the required amount without security other than your promise to pay."

Tremendously relieved yet not knowing whether to be glad or sorry, the girl drew out the Half Moon bank account, signed a thirty-day promissory note for sixteen thousand dollars, and thanked Harmon Truesdale with tears in her Scotch blue eyes. Handing her a canvas sack wrapped in brown paper, so that it appeared to be just an ordinary package, the banker said:

"Incidentally, it will not be necessary to have McKenzie's endorsement on Tedro Ames' note now. You have probably heard—"

"I have," said Fay very shortly and walked hurriedly out. Just as she reached the sidewalk a horseman dashed past shouting at the top of his voice:

"Ab Thurston's been killed at the T A ranch! The Stoddard Brothers, Jake and Len, and Greasy Holderness found Ab 's mornin'. He was shot through the head and Tedro Ames has disappeared and there was an ace of spades on the body!"

The girl stood stone-still, leaning against the bank for support while she saw every store and saloon on Main Street spilling out humanity. Everybody rushed to the spot where a buckboard had halted in front of Coroner Endholm's undertaking establishment. Three riders surrounded this buckboard which was driven by Greasy Holderness. Leonard Stoddard and Jake, mounted, led Greasy's saddle horse.

Rallying, Fay went to her pony, tied the package—containing twenty thousand dollars—in the slicker behind her saddle, swung up and rode to the crowd. Men were taking something all wrapped in a tarpaulin from the buckboard and carrying it into Endholm's place. The crowd was silent listening to Len Stoddard, tall, raw-boned, erect in his saddle and very flint-like of face.

"As most of you know," said Stoddard, "after the

game when I won Tedro Ames' ranch from him, we sent Ab Thurston out to the T A to take charge. Tedro Ames was with Ab. This mornin' as we rid over there we met Holderness. Havin' nothin' to do, he went with us. Ab's body lay just outside the cabin, and Tedro Ames was noticeably missin'."

"Tedro noticeably missin'," a citizen repeated with emphatic significance. "And a black ace found on the murdered man."

"Yes," gritted Stoddard. "Yet I'm not jumpin' to any wild conclusions. Men, we don't know what between midnight and dawn happened out at the T A."

"But," shouted Holderness, "it shore stands to reason as Tedro Ames was mighty sore at these Stoddard boys. Maybe he took out some o' his spite on their foreman, Ab Thurston."

"Why say 'maybe'?" yelled someone. "Tedro done it. He's run. That shows plain—"

A babble of enraged voices interrupted, and Fay could not help biting her lower lip as she heard Tedro denounced. Of course these voices proclaimed young Tedro Ames had murdered Thurston. What was more Tedro must be one of the Black Aces mob. He had put that ace of spades on Thurston's body—after shooting the man in cold blood.

Sheriff Pete Potter stamped out of the undertaking parlor, and sprang up into the buckboard. "Quiet, everybody," he roared, lifting his right hand. "The evidence in this case is pretty conclusive. I'm organizing a posse, or two posses at once, to hunt for Tedro

Ames. Len Stoddard and Jake, I'm deputizing both of you. Who else will volunteer?"

Strangely, Fay thought, when she considered that Tedro had been well liked, more men volunteered to aid the sheriff than he could possibly use. Sick and faint she had turned Torchy, when Leonard M. Stoddard forced his mount through the densely packed crowd to join her.

"Good mornin', Miss Fay," sweeping off his hat. "I see you're not ridin' the famous pinto, Apache, today."

"Len," the girl looked the man straight in his steel-grey eyes, "you don't believe Tedro—?" she stopped.

Stoddard looked away quickly. "Honestly, I don't know what to think. Tracks show that Tedro stooped over Ab's body, and it appeared that Ab was shot as he stood in the cabin door with lamplight behind him. Tedro got his horse and rode into the willows on Twisty Creek. We soon lost his trail. I hope he didn't do it, yet—"

"Yet you think he did," the girl heard herself say. "I'm going home." She wanted to get away from this town where the citizens were so quick to turn against a happy-go-lucky, cheerful josher who'd never been known to harm any man.

Stoddard however reached out and caught her bridle. "Fay, please believe that I'm your friend. I'd hoped someday to be more than a friend, but—"

"But you never can be even a friend—if you turn against Tedro." Fay scarce knew what she was saying.

52

"Eh? He means so much to you then? . . . How'd you like the pinto hoss?"

"Don't mention that horse. I didn't accept it, couldn't accept it from anybody except my own father. And I now hate Apache, hate him."

"Huh?" gasped Stoddard. "Tedro never gave you—?"

"No! But it's none of your business. Len Stoddard, I can't think much of you and your brother for gambling with Tedro and winning his ranch. In fact I think—"

"Someone else would have if we hadn't, Miss Fay. Let me ride home with you, please."

"No. No, thank you. And, don't call on me any more."

"You're talking wild. Sure, I'll come to see you at the Half Moon again. I ain't easy discouraged. Besides I've been deputized and since the sheriff ain't much force, I'm the man everybody is looking to to round up this Black Ace pack. When I get 'em behind the bars, perhaps—"

Fay shook his hand from the bridle and rode away at a lope. Behind her the town buzzed like a beehive. Men were leading saddled horses from both livery stables, others inspecting six-shooters and rifles. Loomis, the hardware man, was dispensing boxes of fresh cartridges. The sheriff's posses were getting ready —to hunt for Tedro Ames.

"Terrible things pile one on top of the other," thought the dismayed girl as she loped along the dusty

53

brown road. "There's never been anything like this in Swiftwater Valley. What, what is going to happen? Did Tedro—? No. He didn't. *Didn't!*"

She was crossing the ford on willow-lined Brush Creek, where yesterday Tedro Ames, unknown to Fay, had traded horses with none other than Wolf Whalen, bandit, before she realized she was so far along the trail, and as she rode out of the willows a masked rider suddenly barred her path.

"Get 'em up, you!"

A pair of wicked eyes peered through the slits of a black mask, and a Colt .45 was aimed menacingly at the girl's face, to enforce the command.

CHAPTER FOUR
THE OUTLAW'S HORSE

Ike Bowlaigs, riding in the rough foothills south and west of the Half Moon ranch, had no idea in mind other than just picking up a few scattered bunches of cattle missed by the fall roundup. Ike "reckoned a hunk o' venison would taste almoughty good to Miz Sandy and her ma and to Ike hisself." Therefore he carried an ancient single-shot buffalo gun, so heavy and so long of barrel that it "were a 'tarnal nuisance to a hossbacker". But Ike had never forsaken "ol' Topsy" in favor of a more modern firearm.

This veteran hand knew about where to find a buck, and tying his horse, stole over a hill through thick aspens. Eventually he peered stealthily into a small, grassy park, crossing which—heading back to the higher country—were no less than seven deer.

Ike Bowlaigs rested ol' Topsy across a hollow log and squinted along the barrel. Wham! The terrific recoil of the formidable weapon knocked him flat on his back, but as he leaped to his feet six deer were vanishing into the jackpines like streaks of light. The seventh, a lordly six-point buck, was down. Ike Bowlaigs had cut the animal's throat and was preparing to "calf dress" it when a bantering voice came out of the nearby pines:

"You slab-sided, spavined-hocked ol' wart-hog, what you mean shooting deer outa season? I'm the game warden and I've snuck up on you."

Ike spun on his boot heels, magpie-sharp eyes darting about. Then abruptly he laughed. "Yah? You'll ha' tuh change yore voice more'n that afore you fool this ol' haid. Fust time you ever snuck up onto anything, Tedro. Also, fust time I ever knowed you to be shakin' yore hoofs this early. Come on out an' I'll give you a hunk o' liver tuh take to yore shanty. You're actually out huntin' fer cattle, er—?"

Out of the pines stepped Tedro, leading his blaze-faced, stocking-legged bay horse. Since he had lost everything in last night's poker game he was now spurless, and instead of his natty calfskin jacket wore an old blue jumper. However, he still had his striped trousers.

But at the sombrero—a black, flat-crowned, dust-

and sweat-streaked old Stetson with torn brim—which covered his curly black head Ike stared in amazement. Tedro had not shaved this morning. His eyes were bloodshot, face flushed, a queer defiant set to his lips.

"When you get an eyeful," he remarked, "I might give you a hand. But so far as takin' a hunk of liver to my shanty—I ain't goin' back there. Daggone yore old hide, you quit me. But you did right. No hard feelings."

"Yes—no—wa-al," Ike began. "Aw, ding bust it, Tedro, I'm fer you still, an' I'd ha' stuck only—only folks was laughin' up their sleeves, behint yore back at—"

"At me," said Tedro in a brittle tone. "I've tumbled at last, and how! The girl threw me down, I've lost my ranch and— You're still my friend, Ike? Won't turn against me?" He gazed at the old puncher almost pathetically.

"Put 'er thar!" Ike extended his gnarled hand. "Dog blast yore wuthless carcass, I al'ays liked you. What you done? Whar'd you get that lid? How'd you lose—?"

"Poker. Didn't give a whoop what happened. Allowed I'd make a stake or go bust proper. Went bust, and what of it? That don't matter, not since Sandy tol' me to ride outa her life. What matters is— Ike, there'll be a posse scourin' the hills fer me. I'm on the dodge."

"How come? Get it off yore chest," ordered the veteran. Skillfully he slit the deer's carcass open with his

56

hunting knife and began to dress it.

Tedro told of what had taken place at the T A last night, concluding: "I allowed I'd have a better show of gettin' the bushwhacker if I was foot loose, 'stead of locked up in the jug, waitin' trial. I figgered somethin' else, too, Ike. We'll have a drink on it."

Untying a slicker-wrapped bundle from his saddle and taking therefrom a quart bottle of whisky, Tedro began to pry at the cork with his knife while Ike whetted his lips in anticipation.

"I figgered," resumed the cowboy, "that since I don't amount to a tinker's damn an' never will I might as well hit the owl-hoot trail."

"Huh? Uh? Uk-unn. Nope! That trail ends with a hemp rope 'round yore gullet."

"What d' I care. Short life and a thrillin' one. Cash to spend. Liquor in towns where you ain't knowed, gamblin', women. Aw, t'hell with the women. I'm off 'em. . . . Ike, I swapped hosses with nobody else than Wolf Whalen hisself yest'day."

"Sw-ap—ped hosses with that outlaw? You're plumb batty. You never—"

"But I did. He wasn't masked neither. Otherwise even I, the laughin'-stock o' Swiftwater, would ha' ben s'picious. I traded Wolf Whalen that damn pinto, Apache, fer this hoss, and I got a bill of sale from 'Horse Trader Markley.' Ain't that good? Very valuable that bill of sale. . . . Daggone this cork. I can't get it loose."

"Hustle up with it. You wet a feller's appetite, then

can't pull a cork. . . . All right, I'll swaller the yarn. You swapped hosses with the notor'ous outlaw. You got a good bronc thar."

"Uh-huh, but Sheriff Potter knows the cayuse and would take a shot at the feller ridin' it, from long range, too. . . . Ike, I allowed this hoss ought to take me to where Wolf's camped. I headed him into the hills, but nothin' doin'. He didn't strike out for no-place. Disappointin' to me, when I 'lowed I'd join forces with Wolf Whalen."

"Gosh all tomahawks! Ferget that notion."

"Forget it? I'm goin' to do it. . . . Here comes the cork at last. . . . Do it, 'cause I'm a fool and a failure." Tedro held out the bottle to Ike, but the old hand did not take it. He stood erect on his warped legs gazing straight into the younger man's eyes.

"I b'lieve you mean it, Tedro. Damn! I could cuss you out, lay you wide open with my tongue. I could yank my hawgleg an' take you in and have you throwed in the hoosegow fer a killin' you didn't do and I could—"

"Have a snorter. Here's to the outlaw trail." Tedro laughed recklessly and upended the bottle, then jerked it away from his lips as old Ike said:

"Kid, would it make any difference if you knowed that Sandy still cares?"

"Does she? Like fun she does!"

"Tedro, the gal cried her eyes out yest'day. By actin' the loco idiot, you broke her heart. Know what'd please her now?"

"What? You ain't kiddin' me? She does care?"

"I'm tellin' you the truth. I've lived a long time and forgot more about people'n you know. Kid—that's all you are, jus' a fool kid, actin' like one now—the thing as'd please Sandy would be fer you to come back."

"What you mean, come back?"

"You know. Get on your mettle, show you got somethin' to you. Make a man of yourself, 'stead o' bein' and actin' a weak-kneed, yella-backed whelp, lackin' the guts tuh face—"

"Shut up!" snapped Tedro. "I'll show you whether I lack guts. Hell! 'Stead of throwin' in with Wolf, I might make a start by capturin' him, uh?"

"You might. S'posin' you show Sandy that—"

"That I ain't a quitter, welsher, counterfeit bum. . . . Ike, you've opened my eyes. If Sandy really cares, that does make a difference! Let's shake again. Wait 'til I get rid of this liquor."

Tedro Ames stepped off some twenty paces, carefully set the bottle down on a stump and backed away from it. Ike did not divine his intention, until he saw the young cowman whip out his six-shooter—Tedro had appropriated Ab Thurston's gun and belt—and fire. With the crash of the report came also the tinkle of shattered glass and raw whisky sprayed an old pine stump.

"Hey," Ike bellowed. "What's the idea wastin' good likker, when I was waterin' at the mouth fer—?"

"That truck gets a man down and keeps him down, Ike. I might as well make the fresh start without its handicap. . . . Still can shoot, can't I?"

"Yeh, yeh. I wish you'd missed. Daggone!"

"Ike, I got to keep hid out, but I'd like mighty much to know what's goin' on at the Half Moon, like word of Sandy particular, also what the Black Aces are doin'. . . . S'posin' I leaves notes for you in the knot hole of that lightnin' blasted lone pine on Wind Ridge and you do the same for me? That'll be our post office."

"I was thinkin' o' the same thing, Tedro. Them Black Aces now, what the heck they mean?"

"I dunno," Tedro shrugged indifferently. He looked younger again, gayer, the old twinkle was back in his eyes. "You might bring some grub, like a loaf of bread and hunk of butter, to the lone pine, too, Ike. I'll help you load the buck on yore hoss and then I'm goin' to Brush Creek where maybeso I can pick up the tracks left by a certain pinto hoss called Apache, now bein' rid by Wolf Whalen bandit with a thousand bucks on his scalp. That thousand'll come in handy fer a starter, Ike, you saddle-warped ol' longhorn, and plumb best friend a chump like me ever had."

Tedro Ames, riding with a new light in his eyes and new purpose in life, was very careful how he crossed the ridges on his long ride to Brush Creek. Several times he thought of going directly to Swiftwater and telling his side of the shooting at the T A, but always the thought that his story would not be credited kept him from doing so. Better be at large, even though he must stay hidden, ride the dim trails and shun society, than be locked up.

Brush Creek flowed into Swiftwater River from the east. Tedro struck the stream half a mile above the ford on the road, and as a matter of precaution he took to the dense willows, riding slowly downstream, searching always for tell-tale tracks left by Apache.

As the cowboy neared the ford his mount suddenly stopped and pricked forward its ears. Though it did not whinny, it glanced around at its rider as much as to say, "Take a look." This was an outlaw's horse and trained not to betray its presence. Tedro was nearly a minute finding what the horse saw or smelled or both. It was another rider waiting behind brush where the road came out of the willows on the south side of the ford. A tall, slender fellow, riding a black horse, he was masked!

"Uh-huh," grunted Tedro and loosened his gun.

Suddenly the masked rider jumped his horse out to bar the road and across the stillness rang a snarled command: "Get 'em up, you!"

"And who's the polecat stickin' up?" thought Tedro, moving his mount out of the brush. Then he saw Fay McKenzie on Torchy. Her right hand had flashed upward; her left controlled her pony. Her face had gone chalk-white. Tedro heard her gasp:

"But you mustn't take—"

"'Nuff o' that, sister. Pile off! Reckon the stuff's tied behint yore saddle."

Tedro was in a quandary. Would the holdup shoot

61

the girl if he, Tedro, spoke? Not likely. He called:

"Talk to me awhile, rattlesnake!"

The man's head and body and gun swiveled around in one motion, and the Colt .45 spat leaden death at Tedro Ames, the bullet whistling past his left ear. Tedro's weapon flamed and roared. Instantly the masked man was reeling drunkenly in his saddle, his arms flailing the air, while his terrified horse sped, unguided, along the edge of the willows.

Like a roper after a calf, Tedro zipped after horse and rider. As he flashed past Fay McKenzie he saw her face and eyes register relief and amazement; heard her astounded, "You, Tedro!" But he did not pause.

Ah, the masked fellow had keeled out of his saddle, his horse tearing onward. Tedro's stocking-legged bay slid to a halt and Tedro landed on his feet, ready to do battle with the fallen man, or—

The cowpuncher swore feelingly. He had wanted to get that jasper alive, but the man, shot through the chest, was dead already. Tedro slipped off the black mask and voiced a dumbfounded ejaculation. Fay dashed up, her mount snorting and shying.

"Who is it, Tedro? . . . Arch Greenwald? Why— why—it can't be!"

"But 'tis Greenwald," said Tedro practically. "Darned sorry I shot—I mean killed—him, but it seemed sorta necessary."

"Oh, it was, it was," cried the girl. "But Arch works for Con Richards and has for years. It don't seem possible that he—"

"Went bronc all of a suddent and decided to stick you up. I ain't no idea why. Blunt fact is, Arch did go haywire and I seen him and— Hear that drum and pound of hoofs, Sandy? Beg pardon, I should say Miss McKenzie since—since yesterday."

"Tedro," the girl's eyes were more frightened than they had been when she was facing the holdup's gun. "What we hear is Sheriff Potter and a posse, coming from town. They're looking for you!"

"Uh-huh, and they're in the willows, splashin' 'cross the ford right now." Tedro Ames grinned at Fay, in his eyes—those twinkling eyes which had always laughed at life and now laughed at danger—the old familiar reckless light. "As the Texans say, I'll light a shuck," he added. Jabbing the mask into his pocket he caught his saddle horn with one hand and vaulted to the saddle without touching stirrup.

"Glad to ha' seen you again, Sandy. Adios." The curly-headed rider with the slouchy black hat and the old blue jumper was gone. Out of the willows, forty yards up stream, galloped Sheriff Potter with five possemen.

Seeing the stocking-legged bay horse leaving the vicinity with the speed of an antelope, the sheriff yelled: "That's Wolf Whalen's hoss, boys. Bet Wolf's ridin' 'im. No wonder we heard shootin'. After 'im, fellers!"

The posse was already after Tedro as fast as they could lash their mounts. Five men went zipping past Fay McKenzie and the body of Arch Greenwald, and

63

two of the five were shooting with rifles. But as Fay saw Tedro's bay swerve into the brush and vanish instantly, she breathed easier.

Sheriff Potter had pulled up. His eyes like saucers he was gaping at her, at the body. "Greenwald? Dead? We heard shots. What ha—?"

"You didn't see it?" asked Fay a bit shakily.

"Nope."

"Well, this Greenwald, masked, held me up with a gun, and—"

"Arch Greenwald held you up. You're talkin' through yore hat."

"That'll do, Sheriff. Folks don't tell a McKenzie she is lying. Greenwald held me up. Tedro Ames broke out of the brush. They exchanged shots. Greenwald missed, Tedro didn't. Get this straight. Tedro was more than justified in—"

"Tedro?" yelled the sheriff. "Where's he now? Was he ridin' that bay?"

"Yes, and—"

"He was, was he? Ridin' Wolf Whalen's hoss! Strikes me as darned significant, and also very simple. Tedro Ames has joined the outlaws, if he ain't been one of 'em all the time. Ridin' Wolf's hoss? Must be one o' Wolf's favorites."

"I don't understand what you're talking about," the girl began, her eyes flashing hot anger. But the sheriff was loping to join his man hunters.

There was nothing Fay could do, so she touched Torchy with her quirt and dashed away toward the

Half Moon, hoping and praying that Tedro would not be caught.

She need not have worried for Tedro Ames' present safety. His horse, an outlaw's horse, went through the willows like a jack rabbit, twisting, dodging, turning around clumps of brush so swiftly that even the expert rider in the saddle was put to it to stay aboard. A fence running across the willows bothered the bay not at all. It merely hopped over it and went on. This horse knew far more about evading man hunters than his rider.

Thus Tedro was soon at Swiftwater River, while the posse floundered helplessly about in the brush a mile to rearward. Fording the swift, clear stream he took to the rough hills between river and mountains. Now that the excitement was over he was sleepy, hungry, dog-weary, for he had had neither sleep nor rest the previous night. He climbed up on a ridge densely forested, and with a wisp of grass curried his bay, of which he was becoming very fond, from ears to hoofs, then picketed the horse in an open glen, and bedding down with his saddle blanket he went soundly to sleep. His last waking thought was that he had made a mighty good start towards a come-back. Good old Ike Bowlaigs. 'Twas just providential that he had met Ike this morning.

Shortly after sundown Tedro awakened numb, cold and ravenously hungry. He had killed no small game for food, had nothing with him except salt and coffee.

Why not go to a ranch and get a square meal? The town was against him, the sheriff hunting him, but surely he still had friends among the cowmen. The old timers never turned against a fellow unless they were mighty sure they had good reasons. Henry Kline, one of the real old settlers, lived alone up north a few miles. Tedro would call on ol' Henry.

Darkness had been upon the rough country for an hour when the fugitive cowpuncher approached the H K, connected, on Burnt Fork. Yet as he rode nearer he made out a human figure stealing northward up the hill away from the buildings. Atop this hill, in a small open area, Tedro knew Kline's salting ground to be.

Consumed with curiosity the cowboy circled, gained the crest of the hill ahead of the man on foot, and hid in a cluster of aspens. When the furtive figure drew near, Tedro stepped out, a cocked six-shooter in his hand.

The man froze in his tracks. "Here 'tis," he exclaimed. "Don't shoot. I got 'er fer you. Take it an' get." He was thrusting a heavy sack at thunderstruck Tedro Ames.

Thunderstruck because he had now recognized old Henry Kline. "What the devil you want me to take, Henry?" asked Tedro inelegantly, as he holstered his gun.

The old timer's eyes ran up and down the cowboy's body, finally resting on his face under the black hat. "Am I seein' Tedro Ames?"

"Nobody else, Henry. Who was you expectin' to—"

As though by magic four men lifted themselves up out of the sagebrush, instantly forming a half-circle around Kline and Tedro. They were darkly clad, wearing big black hats and black masks; one an unusually big fellow. Starlight glinted on the blued metal of four six-shooters. A lean, wiry man spoke in a waspish voice:

"We'll take the sack, Mister Kline, and jus' tuh keep yore nosey friend and you from follerin' us, we'll tie you up."

"Hey, we ain't honin' to be tied none," said Tedro. "Who are you?"

"That's fer us to know and you to find out," rasped he of the waspish voice—an assumed voice, Tedro decided. "Keep yore hands reachin' or you'll stop a lot of lead."

"I believe you," said Tedro and because two guns covered him while a third man proceeded to tie him solidly with a lariat to one of the largest aspens at the edge of the grove, he made no resistance. Nor did Henry Kline offer any objections, when he also was lashed to a tree.

The four men took the small sack Kline had been carrying, looked into it, felt of its contents and then three of them disappeared as silently and as magically as they had appeared. But the fourth man went in among the aspens, where very soon Tedro heard the rustle of leaves under the hoofs of his horse. This sound soon died away to be replaced by the sound of hoofbeats on firm soil.

"They've taken my hoss, Henry," observed Tedro. "Just when I was gettin' mighty fond of that bay nag. Had even named him Bandit."

"Can't see how you can speak so ca'm like," snorted the ranchman and burst into lurid profanity, cursing the four masked men for blacklegs, bloodsuckers, killers. "And double blankety blank it, Tedro, if you hadn't showed up I'd ha' been a heap better off. Don't figger them skunks would ha' snubbed me to a tree. Now we're both tied."

"Liable to stay here fer the night anyhow," said Tedro. "Ye-ah, judgin' by the way this rope's cuttin' into my hide, we're stayin' right here 'til somebody finds us, Henry. I used to be able to sleep in any position, but I never tried it standin' back again' a rough tree, with four—five knots gougin' me and a lariat—"

"Anyhow them blasted Black Aces didn't kill us," growled old Henry.

"Black Aces?" asked Tedro quickly.

"Uh-huh." Kline told of the threat he had received, of his raising cash and starting out to put it in his salt trough on the salting ground for his cattle. "Met you afore I reached the place. . . . I 'membered vivid as Smith was bushwhacked and I wanted to keep livin' fer a spell yet. Fer long enough to put the kibosh on this dirty, underhanded, night-workin' herd o'—" Profanity.

68

"I got one of them spade aces myself," remarked Tedro. "Nothin' on it, though."

"You got one! That's funny. Funny 'cause this pack seems to know what they're about and how could they expect to get any dough from you?"

"So that's what they're after—money," said Tedro thoughtfully. "Henry, this is all-fired queer. I wasn't asked to dig up, yet the only reason I'm still alive is because Ab Thurston, wearin' my big white Stetson, was standin' plain in the lamplight at my cabin, 'stead of me. At least that's the way I dope it out. . . . The killer, hid in the brush, and quite a distance from his man, made a mistake."

"Why the devil would anybody want to shoot you, Tedro? Why nobody'd pay you the compliment of considerin' you dangerous."

"Can't always tell from the looks of a cayuse how hard he can buck," drawled Tedro. "Probably s'prise you to larn I've drawn first blood for our side."

A derisive snort was the vitriolic old ranchman's reply to this. He then asked Tedro to tell him the truth of how Ab Thurston had died. "I heard in town as you done it, but thunder, I never believed that."

"Glad you didn't, Henry." Tedro related exactly what had occurred at the T A.

"So. Well you made a chump of yourself by high-tailin'. Tedro, my lad, I'm fer you, but I dunno how you can square yourself now."

"That's easy. Get the walloper as did it. . . . I kinder suspect Wolf Whalen's outlaws are back of all this hell

69

raisin'. I aimed to track Wolf himself on a pinto hoss I traded him, but afore I could find the trail somethin' happened to interfere terrible with that plan. Now I ain't got no hoss a-tall and I'm snubbed to a Quaker with the rope eatin' into my belly what's lank as a greyhound's, and—"

"Lissen, Tedro," snorted Kline. "I can't believe that any bunch of outlaws would ever start playin' such a coyote game as these Black Aces are playin'. No sir. It jus' don't stand to reason. If Wolf wanted cash why wouldn't he go after it in real bandit style? Rob the bank in Swiftwater. If and when we ever uncover this spade-ace trail we won't find no bandits ridin' it."

"Maybe you're right," agreed Tedro. "The skunk I shot t'day—he was stickin' up Sandy, for some reason —was none other than Arch Greenwald."

"Greenwald? Well, I'll be—. You killed him?"

"Sorry, but I did. . . . Do I hear somebody comin'?"

"Aw, nobody'll pass this way afore noon tomorrow and by then we'll be so nigh dead that it'll take us a week to get on our feet again. . . . Uh-ah! Horses!!"

Three men, riding slowly, materialized out of the darkness. Their objective seemed to be the aspen grove. One rider was big of frame, broad-shouldered, unusually tall and seeing him rather clearly in the starlight Henry Kline voiced an oath of astonishment, then boomed:

"'Lo, there, Harmon Truesdale. What you doin'?"

Instantly the three horsemen reined up. They seemed suspicious, wary. One held a rifle ready for use; the others cocked six-shooters.

"Who's speaking?" demanded the deep voice of the Swiftwater banker.

Kline told him who was speaking and tersely explained the situation. "Get us loose, pronto, Truesdale. How come you're here?"

As the three men rode closer, Tedro saw that the banker's companions were Loomis, the hardware man and "Mooch," a ratty-eyed grub-line rider who put in most of his time "mooching" in town.

"By George, we seem to have arrived too late," said Truesdale as he released Kline. "Answering your question, Henry, you had told me where you were to put the money. And though I knew you wouldn't consent to my interfering, I nevertheless decided to make an attempt to catch the scoundrels after your cash. So I got two good men and—"

"But you're over an hour—seems like six hours we been tied—too daggoned late," rumbled the ranchman. "Yet double do-dangle it, are we glad tuh see you!" Old Henry stamped his feet and beat his numbed hands together.

"Hey, Loomis, take this rope offen me," called Tedro.

"Wait," commanded Truesdale. "Tedro Ames, I do not know how you happen to be here, but it is plainly my duty to take you to jail. Kline, you've heard, Tedro is accused of—"

"Hell's fire, yes," the ranchman interrupted. "Tedro's gone bronc proper."

71

While Tedro considered what seemed an amazing statement from a friend, the banker resumed: "Did you know a black ace of spades was found on Thurston's body?"

"What's that?" ejaculated Tedro. "An ace of spades on Thurston's body?"

"Yes. Did you put it there?"

"Huh?" growled the cowpuncher. "I wish I'd made a pretense of ridin' off and then come coyotin' back to the T A. I'd likely have caught me a Black Ace plantin' his card on a victim. Daggone. From here out I won't overlook any bets."

"Not likely you'll have a chance to overlook any bets, as you put it," Truesdale resumed. "Kline, I was about to tell you that there is a second very serious charge against this fellow. One of Sheriff Potter's possemen dashed into town late this afternoon reporting that at the ford on Brush Creek, Tedro Ames attempted to hold up Miss Fay McKenzie. He was only prevented from doing so by the timely arrival of Arch Greenwald."

Tedro could scarcely believe his ears. "Who said so?" he demanded.

"In the ensuing gun battle, Tedro Ames shot and killed Greenwald. Potter with five men heard the shots, arrived a few minutes later, but in time to prevent Ames from robbing Miss McKenzie, for, naturally, Tedro fled for his life."

"Is that Sheriff Potter's version?" asked Tedro very quietly.

"Yes," said the banker. "The man who brought this word to Swiftwater stated further that beyond any reasonable doubt Tedro Ames is allied with Wolf Whalen's outlaws. He was riding a certain marked horse known by the sheriff to be Wolf Whalen's customary mount."

"Provin' an old saw," said Tedro calmly, "to the effect that a feller should never swap hosses blindfolded. I ride an outlaw's hoss, so I've joined the bandits, well, well. And 'cause Greenwald was known to be a square rannie, I, not Greenwald, was the holdup man and I murdered Greenwald. The sheriff's conclusions do him great credit. Brainy man, Pete Potter. Wonder what Sandy said?"

"Therefore, Mr. Kline," Truesdale was going on, "you see that we must take Tedro in."

The grizzled old rancher grunted, nodded, muttered something into his uncombed beard. Then: "Them four snakes as robbed me, tied both of us, was afoot, but they took Tedro's hoss. . . . So you fellers—I'm shore 'bliged to you—will need a hoss to take Tedro tuh town. Let's go to my shanty and get one of mine."

"And take the prisoner with us," suggested Loomis.

Tedro was untied. Two six-shooters menaced him. He was ordered to walk down the sagebrush hill to Kline's dark buildings. Arrived there, old Henry entered the stable, lighted a lantern and backed a dun horse out of a stall. He started to saddle it. Directly outside the door Loomis held the three saddle horses of the Truesdale party. Mooch kept his gun on Tedro while the banker, standing in the door, conversed with Kline. It seemed Harmon Truesdale, in cooperation with the sheriff and all honest citizens, was already doing all in his power to apprehend the infamous organization self-styled Black Aces.

"I'm out for blood myself!" snapped Kline, when something happened outside the barn. The dull smack of a fist driving home; the roar of an exploding gun.

Kline whirled to see Mooch, the runt, lifted bodily by Tedro's fist and slammed to the floor of the stable; his six-shooter belching fire and smoke as he hit the planks. Truesdale had turned toward the cyclone which was Tedro Ames and reached for his Colt. But Tedro's left fist smashed the banker squarely in his left eye.

Truesdale dropped to his knees, his gun cleared leather. Tedro caught the weapon by the barrel, twisted it from the big man's fingers, then pivoted and launched himself at Boyd Loomis. All this in sliced seconds. Henry Kline saw the Colt in Tedro's hands descend on Loomis' head and with his gun half drawn, Loomis fell as though hit by an axe. Up on Truesdale's horse and chasing the other two horses ahead of him, Tedro was gone into the dark night with a ring and drum of hoofs.

Grizzled old Henry Kline leaped out of the stable and emptied a six-shooter after racing horses and racing rider. Strange that his bullets cut only empty air when Kline was considered a dead shot. Yet per-haps not strange considering the exultant thought running through the old timer's mind:

"By—! Tedro's woke up at last. He shore done noble!"

He looked at Mooch and Loomis. Both were out cold. He looked at banker Truesdale, leaning against the door jamb, holding one hand to his left eye and appearing woozy and sick indeed. But what Henry Kline said to Truesdale, as that gentleman rallied, and what he actually thought were very different things.

Kline said: "That's jus' too daggone bad and the only hoss I got caught up can't run fer sour apples!"

CHAPTER FIVE

SHOCK ON SHOCK

As on the two preceding mornings Fay McKenzie was waiting for Hank Farnum's stage. Waiting and scanning the road as yesterday evening after she had reached home following her adventure at Brush Creek, she had scanned the road to southward looking, looking for the old Half Moon chuck wagon, the horse cavvy and the cowpunchers to appear out of the distant horizon.

She had thought not only would it give her a sense of security, but it would be a tremendous relief to have the reliable, tried and true cowpunchers and Foreman Jess Walker once more on the ranch. Jess had a level head, had been on Half Moon for fifteen long years.

Fay and her father both placed the utmost dependence upon this lean, hard-as-nails, rawhide-faced old cow foreman. Perhaps Jess would know what to do in this crisis. At least he could comfort the girl with his sage advice. Not for a minute could the troubled girl get out of her mind the terrible threat of the Black Aces. Was she doing the right thing? Was it necessary to pay to those unknown killers twenty thousand dollars? No small amount for any cow outfit to raise. Its loss would not actually break the Half Moon, but it would cripple the outfit.

However, the girl had looked in vain. No dust cloud had heralded the coming home of the Half Moon cowboys from shipping beef at Harpoon. And the night had passed without their riding in. Now on Saturday morning, the morning of the day when Fay was to place twenty thousand dollars at the foot of the lightning-blasted lone pine on Wind Ridge, the stage came rattling around the bend and Hank Farnum cracked his whip, then drew his team to a brake-squealing halt beside the waiting girl.

" 'Lo, Sandy. Reckon you don't need no mail box. Still I does snatch the sack out of it of evenin's as I come by on the return trip. Here you be, and there's yet another extra hot off Ray Thomas' press. Ray's got that ol' printin' machine jus' a-smokin'. Extra yest'day, 'nother this mornin'."

"What's the news, Hank?"

"Plenty, but you can read it in the paper. Wa-al, one thing as ain't in there I might tell you, private like,

76

'though I ain't tellin' it nowheres else. Yest'day I brung up from Harpoon the biggest wad o' cash fer Harmon Truesdale I ever did bring to his bank."

"Yes?"

"Uh-huh. Don't say boo, Sandy, but it looks like Harmon is gettin' set to do the right thing by ranchers and merchants and saloon keepers what finds 'emselves honored by cards from the Black Aces. . . . Uckoo, matter, Sandy? You get one of them black cards, too?"

"Never mind, Hank. Did Charlie, the driver on the Harpoon end, happen to say anything about seein' our outfit?"

"Nope, he didn't. . . . Sandy, I'm goin' to have some punkins for a passenger on my back trip 's evenin'."

"Who?"

"A United States Deputy Marshal. Uh-huh, the post-master's sent for this feller, 'cause threats—them spade-ace threats—are bein' sent through the mail and Postmaster Jim Knowlton said he had a right to get a man on the job to look into it. A daggoned ser'us matter for whoever's misusin' the U. S. mails if he gets catched. And the post office department never quits huntin' for a crook."

"Oh, good. Good!" exclaimed Fay. "Now we'll have somebody on the job who knows how to handle such a queer, terrible situation. . . . So long, Hank."

The girl dumped on the ground the contents of the mail sack and fearing that she might find another square, pink envelope, looked at the letters and papers. She was suddenly aware that she was holding her breath, which rushed out in a long sigh of relief as no pink envelope came to light. But here was something both interesting and alarming, a plain white envelope, the penciled address on it scarcely legible. "Sandy—Half Moon Ranch; Swiftwater, Colo."

Fay knew that scrawl. Foreman Jess Walker's long suit was neither writing nor spelling. She ripped open the envelope and read:

"Dere Sandy This is Friday mornin an I jus got tiem toe git this in mail we put wheels under the steers yesday evenin and the ol man went with em coupla yahos burned him fer pases an went long—s morning I get telgram from ol Bill over to a water tank town called Prary Owl nigh kansas line.—Bill giv orders to telegraf man to catch me with the mesage sure pop—it sed—Met Denis Holmes cattleman here stop bought thousand yearlins from him stop you bring whole outfit get this herd immediately stop trail em home—
That was the dope Sandy and Im takin' wagon cavvy and cowboys and headin fer Prary Owl loked on r r map and towns bout 225 miles lok fer us wen you see us—better get help and vacnate them calves in west pasture afore blakleg gets mong em

yors Jess Walker."

Fay sat down abruptly on a convenient sagebrush

and gazed at the letter with dismayed concern. Her father had bought a thousand yearlings and wired Jess to come and get them. Somehow it didn't seem as if Bill McKenzie would have bought more cattle with winter coming and the Half Moon already stocked with all the cattle it could feed. But her father must have done this and—this was what dismayed the girl—the cowboys would not be home today, tomorrow, next day or even next week. Thus when the greatest problem and crisis of her life confronted the girl she was deprived of help. It was a crushing blow. Oh if only her father, Jess and the half dozen rollicky, reckless, fight-loving rannies were on the job here at the Half Moon. Fay firmly believed that they would not be long in running to earth the dread Black Aces. But now—

She felt so helpless, so hopeless, so very much alone. Ike Bowlaigs was some help and comfort, but not a great deal. How about Tedro? He certainly had helped her yesterday. Yet any man would have under the same circumstances. Fay had sent him out of her life. He could not be expected to volunteer any aid now. Besides he was a fugitive, hiding in the hills and she had no way of getting in touch with him. (Ike had not told Fay of his meeting Tedro and of their post office arrangement.)

Mechanically the girl glanced at the other letters. Nothing of importance. She picked up the "extra" of the *Swiftwater Star* and the headline leaped at her eyes:

"TEDRO AMES BRANDED OUTLAW!"

The gist of the story below this lurid title was the same version of the holdup of Fay McKenzie and shooting of Arch Greenwald that Harmon Truesdale had related to Tedro and Henry Kline last night. Fire flashed in Fay's blue, blue eyes. She sprang to her feet whispering fiercely:

"I'm going right to town, find Sheriff Potter and blister him with my tongue. The idea of his making out that I lied! That Tedro was the bandit and Greenwald the man who interfered. I'll make that chump, Potter, retract his statement."

On second and cooler thought, however, she decided she would be acting melodramatic and perhaps a bit ridiculous. What else was in the paper?

"FRANK R. CARTER SHOT!"

Another shock coming right on the heels of the first to the girl of the Half Moon. She read:

"At four this morning, Noisy Ned, cowpuncher of the Circle C, dashed into the sleeping village, aroused Doctor Sterrit and hustled him out to the Circle C to attend Noisy's wounded employer the veteran and esteemed rancher, Frank Carter.

"Ye Editor knew nothing of this until the return of Dr. Sterrit to our midst as daylight was breaking. Doc burst into our sleeping quarters and poured out the following story which he thought should be given publicity for the benefit of all honest citizens. We emphatically agree.

"It seems cowman Frank Carter—you all know his character, rough, gruff, plain spoken, belligerent and obstinate—(I'm not libeling you, Frank. It's the truth.) had received on Wednesday a certain pink envelope containing a certain playing card which we are all beginning to view with alarm and dread. Carter's Ace of Spades in this case—he had received a plain one earlier—bore this message written with pen and ink in a small, delicate hand:

" 'Put twelve thousand dollars, cash, at the foot of the big granite boulder in the center of the open park due south of your ranch before eight o'clock on Friday night. Fail to do this or attempt to trap us and you will be shot. Black Aces.'

"Frank Carter told his men of this demand, exploded to the effect that he'd be blankety-blanked if he'd do anything of the kind, and with his cowboy crew, Noisy, Bug, and Slim Shafter, he took to the woods immediately after nightfall in an attempt to round up any person who might visit the granite boulder hoping there to pick up twelve thousand dollars.

"Noisy, Bug and Slim say it was the spookiest job they ever was on. But no phantom of the night appeared stealing like a night hunting cat toward the big rock. About midnight Carter and his men decided there was no use waiting longer and returned to the Circle C. The cowboys were nervous and apprehensive. Noisy says openly that an Ace of Spades spooks him somethin' terrible. Slim and Bug say they're not superstitious, but—

"(A lot of us are that way. We're not superstitious, but—) Carter scoffed at his men's fears. 'Twas all a d— bluff. A bluff anybody with guts would call. In fact he had called it and nothing had happened.

"The four men, Carter and his three punchers, reached the ranch house, entered and lighted a lamp. Carter stepped to the window to pull down the blind. Thus some unknown assassin without could plainly see him through the window with the lamplight behind him. A shot ripped the silence of the starlit night. A tinkle of shattered glass; a bullet tearing into a human body. Frank Carter yelled: 'I've been shot!' and reeled across the floor and dropped.

"Stunned for a moment, the cowpunchers rallied. Slim blew out the lamp. The three rushed outside, guns ready. No trace of the assassin could they find. Slim quickly returned to the house and ministered to his boss. Fortunately the bullet had missed Carter's lungs and heart. He is wounded badly, but is not in a critical condition, so Doc Sterrit reports.

"But, friends and neighbors, don't try to tell obstinate and defiant old Frank Carter that the

Black Aces are bluffing. Don't try to tell Slim, Noisy or Bug that this mysterious, dread organization don't mean business. The waddies are sticking on the ranch only because of their loyalty to their employer. Needless to say they are guarding Carter, also his wife, every minute. The Circle C is an armed camp, with a sentry posted."

Fay McKenzie looked out across the rolling sagebrush hills west from the Half Moon in the beautiful valley of Swiftwater River where Trail Rest Creek flowed into it. Her throat felt constricted, hot, dry, as if she could never swallow again. Oh, she had done right to raise the cash demanded by these horrid, murderous Black Aces. Yet she felt a tremendous relief that Carter had not actually been murdered. He was gruff and rough and obstinate as Ray Thomas had said, but he was one of the old timers, made of fighting stuff and a "plumb good Injun." It was like him to have called the Black Aces' bluff—which was no bluff.

She turned the front page of the extra and found that editor Thomas had yet more news.

"A CALL TO ARMS!" Thomas headed this column.

"Our erstwhile peaceful locale is in the grip of terrorists. Rise, citizens, and run these unknown wolves to earth. Stamp out this menace. Our valorous Sheriff Potter is on the job. He has not slept in forty-eight hours. In the saddle almost constantly he is leading a posse which is combing the rough hills, seeking the lair of Wolf Whalen's outlaws. When he finds this he believes he will have found also the headquarters of the dread, mysterious Black Aces.

"Leonard M. Stoddard, the iron-faced rancher who knows no fear, is leading a second posse of man hunters. We have not heard from Len since he left town yesterday morning. But we know he'll get results. His brother, Jake, would be riding too, only one must stay at the ranch. Good men, these Stoddards.

"Yesterday afternoon, Sheriff Potter, following his failure to capture Tedro Ames, outlaw, (Ted we never dreamed such a cheery, don't-give-a-hoot waddie as you would take that turn.) sent word to town for everyone to be on the lookout for a certain marked horse—a blood bay with white stocking legs and blaze face. Potter knows this horse did belong to the infamous outlaw, Wolf Whalen. But Tedro Ames was seen riding this identical horse,—one thing which brands Tedro as an outlaw.

"However later information given us by our foremost citizen, Harmon H. Truesdale, reveals that Tedro Ames no longer rides the stocking-legged bay. We learned that last night with two companions our banker took horse and rode the range seeking these human wolves that move in

84

the dark and shoot from the dark.

"What Harmon Truesdale discovered we do not know. He visited our sanctum this morning early and said tersely gruff: 'Tell everybody that Tedro Ames is now riding my steel-grey horse, Charon. Tell your readers that I personally offer one thousand dollars reward for that bandit—alive or dead!'

"How Tedro Ames (incidentally he is easily our most notorious horse trader) acquired Charon we do not know. Mr. Truesdale's left eye, swollen shut, was very black. Generally the most unruffled of men, he seemed to be in a violent temper and when we ventured a question, he froze us with a frigid glare from his one good orb and stalked out."

Fay McKenzie crumpled the paper and looked up once again. "What an ugly, ugly mess," she whispered tight-lipped. "Truesdale, the leading citizen of Swiftwater and the man to whom I am indebted for a loan of sixteen thousand dollars, now offers a reward of one thousand dollars for the man I—yes, I love him. For the man I love—alive or dead!

"Truesdale returns to Swiftwater sporting a black eye and a violent temper. Tedro is now riding Truesdale's steel-grey, Charon. Somebody please tell me what it means?"

The squeak of wagon wheels and the plod of hoofs announced the approach of a team and rig. Fay lifted herself to her booted feet and stood by the mail box watching this plodding outfit draw nearer. An ancient covered wagon drawn by four lumbering horses, a bearded man on the seat with a rifle resting across his knees, his tattered hat pushed back and a wild light in his eyes. At the left of the wagon rode a boy of about eighteen, a rifle across his saddle fork. Behind the vehicle another rider some two years younger, riding a pot-bellied mare with a colt tagging her, and gripping a small rifle in his right hand.

Fay could not see inside the wagon, but she guessed Grandma Elmswood and Mrs. Elmswood and four little kiddies were there. For the man was Jerry Elmswood and his two older sons rode the horses.

" 'Lo?" greeted the girl. "Travelin' or goin' somewhere?"

The team stopped. The two boys glanced behind them apprehensively. The man fingered his beard and a sheepish expression mingled with a sort of sullen defiance spread over his rough features.

"We're leavin'," he muttered.

"Leaving?"

A woman's head half-hidden by a huge sunbonnet suddenly lifted from behind the seat. Her face was a tired face, sad, lined. She said, "Hyar, Fay McKenzie? . . . Yep, we're shovin' out. 'Tain't no place fer young-uns when their pa's likely to meet up with a dry-gulcher's bullet any minute."

"You mean—?" Fay began feeling a sort of dismal emptiness. "Why, Mrs. Elmswood, you had a nice place started, good land, little herd of cows, were making a go of it."

"So we was, an' it shore do tear at us all to up an' get like we're gettin'. But Pa, he got two o' them there spade aces, and he was to town an' he heard tell—"

"Oh, oh! Good gracious, what did the—the devils want of *you folks?*"

"Five hun'red dollars! Much as the place's wuth. Aw, shucks, Miz Mac. I'll tell ye, but doan let it go a past ye—we is shovin' out till the ruckus is over an' done with. Then we's comin' back."

"And a good idea," exclaimed Fay. "But I hope everybody won't run and—"

"More'n us is in the same notion, though," said the woman. "Me an' Grandma jus' cudn't let Pa git shot. Whar's yore Pa? Plenty safe yet, 'cause he's shippin' we heard tell."

"Yuh're lucky, Miz Fay," called one boy. "Ain't got nawthin' tuh worrit 'bout."

"Ged up," said Elmswood.

"Good luck and be sure to come back," called Fay and under her breath, "Oh, no, I've got nothing to worry about. Nothing! But I guess they've got more. Isn't it a crying shame that hard-working, honest people are forced to leave the home they've just built? What can I do about all this?"

She folded the paper and shoved it in her pocket along with Jess Walker's letter, then went to the house where she said nothing of what was troubling her to her mother or to W. T. S. J. Brown, nor did she show either of them the newspaper or the letter. Mrs. McKenzie would worry dreadfully, the negro cook would run to town and try to hide himself where there were lots of people, afraid "them Black Aces'd cast a spell on him."

Five minutes later Ike Bowlaigs rode into the yard and Fay hurried out to meet him at the stable. Ike eased his old buffalo gun to the ground, clambered stiffly off himself.

"I been cuttin' fer sign like you tol' me, Miz Sandy, but I didn't find hide ner hair ner track o' them hell-twisters. Too bad, 'cause tracks is the onliest way I see we are goin' to get wise to them jaspers."

"Ike, I want you to take a real fast horse and shove the wind to Harpoon. Here's a letter from Jess Walker." She told what was in the letter, continued: "Take it with you so you'll be sure to get the name of that town, Prairie Owl, and the cowman's name that Daddy's supposed to have bought the yearlings from.

"You're to reach Harpoon as quick as possible or quicker. Wire Daddy. I think you'll catch him at the point where he'll feed the steers. Ask him if he bought a thousand yearlings from Dennis Holmes at Prairie Owl? Tell him to wire reply at once. Important."

"You doan think he bought 'em," said Ike.

"I think I smell a rat. . . . Wait for his answer, Ike. If it's 'yes', I suppose everything is O.K. But if it's 'no', you're to get hold of Jess Walker by wire somehow—I think the trail he'll take will follow the railroad and you can wire half a dozen stations and get the operators to send men out to locate our cowboys.

"Tell Jess it's a ruse of some kind and tell him to bring the outfit home faster than—"

"Come home hellity-larrup," said Ike. "I get you. Likewise I savvy jus' what's in the back o' yore pretty noodle."

Fay smiled at the old range hand. "But not everything that's in my noodle, Ike. . . . The paper says they accuse Tedro of being a bandit and Truesdale has offered a thousand dollars reward for him."

"You don't say. I never did care overly fer bankers. Kinder beginnin' tuh hate that feller. . . . But doan you worry 'bout 'em ever catchin' up with Tedro. He knows the rough country inside out. . . . I'll be driftin'. 'Less that cattle deal's on the level we're goin' to have some help here what is help."

When Ike had vanished with a wave of his hand, the day dragged endlessly for Fay. Imagined fears were none the less harrowing because they were imaginary. Perhaps not strangely her greatest fear was for Tedro's safety. She wished he would come to the ranch and feared that if he did someone would catch him there. But no one came and save for a couple of freight outfits creeping along the road bound from Harpoon to Swiftwater, the highway was deserted. All seemed serene at the ranch. The blacksmith's whistle and the ring of his hammer were cheery notes. The two ranch hands whistled and sang as they worked in the big meadow finishing up the fencing of haystacks. Little did they know of the tumult in Fay's mind. Little did Mrs. McKenzie know of it either and the older woman thought it nothing out of the ordinary when at sundown Fay announced, as casually as possible, that she was going for a ride.

For a ride with twenty thousand dollars tied behind her saddle—the price for her father's life! Her heart was beating like a trip hammer, her eyes straining themselves into the gathering shadows of night, as she crossed a small stream and climbed the wooded slope leading to the crest of Wind Ridge.

The ridge was forested on either edge, but its crest was utterly barren, save for the lonesome lightning-blasted pine. Fay saw no skulking figures anywhere, though the mournful howl of a coyote startled her immensely. She laughed at herself for being afraid of that moon song, rode on, reached the lone tree. She rode around it to make sure no one was concealed behind it, stepped down, untied her slicker, placed the heavy canvas sack at the foot of the tree and mounting raced away for home, looking back.

The girl had reached the edge of the ridge, almost to the timber when she saw across the barren expanse a rider coming from the other side and loping steadily toward the lone pine. She reined into the timber, watched as though fascinated. Steadily the fading light grew dimmer, but as the man drew nearer to the tree Fay recognized the horse and then the rider.

All the blood seemed to drain from the girl's veins leaving her like a block of ice. That big, powerful, superb gray horse was Harmon H. Truesdale's Charon! The black-hatted rider wearing the dark jumper was Tedro Ames! He halted, stepped from his saddle, stooped and lifted the sack of money. Fay whirled her pony, and gouged it cruelly with her spurs, one thought driving all others from her mind.

"Tedro was the messenger sent to get that money! He was a Black Ace!"

CHAPTER SIX

HARD TO HOLD

Tedro Ames had not even caught sight of Fay McKenzie on Wind Ridge. Riding from the west to reach his objective, Tedro had been so eager to get a message from Ike Bowlaigs; to leave one for Ike also, that he had paused for only a moment to scan the open area from the security of the timber. Seeing no one, he had ventured to lope directly to the lightning-blasted lone pine.

Twilight was fading out to darkness as the young cowpuncher stepped from his saddle—more correctly banker Harmon H. Truesdale's fine flower-stamped and silver-mounted saddle—and gaped in amazement at the canvas sack at the foot of the tree. He untied the draw string, opened the sack. Money!

Written on a white card which lay atop gold coins and crisp bills was:

"Here you are, Black Aces. Now be sure you lay off. Fay McKenzie."

Tedro grunted after his habit, replaced the card, tied the sack and set it down quickly. His gaze swept the vicinity. Likely even now that one or more of those dread Black Aces was watching him. His impulse was to take the cash, but that would not do, for obviously the terrorists had threatened the Half Moon and they had a grim way of backing up their threats with hot lead. Better by far to let them have the money than to place Fay or her father or mother in terrible danger.

Stepping around the tree Tedro caught sight of what he had come to find, an envelope in a knot hole about head high, and there was still sufficient light for him to read in Ike Bowlaigs' scrawl:

"im shovin th wind t harpoon sandys orders she doan think the ol man bought no dogies im t wire him an if he didn ill wire jess t cum home ahellin heres jess leter t splain t you mebe you seen th paper she were ful o stuff aint nothin fer me t tell you but wish youd tell me how truesdale got a black eye an you got his hoss"

That was all. Tedro crumpled the note savagely.

"Why you daggoned old spavin-brained coot," he growled. "Nothin' to tell me! Didn't Fay tell you she'd been threatened and she was puttin' out this big wad? Didn't you tell her this tree was our post office? If you had of— Hum? guess she'd ha' put it here just the same—if this is where she was told to put it."

Of course he could leave no message here for Ike now, and it behooved him to be getting far away from this lone tree immediately. Yet he lingered to read Foreman Jess Walker's letter to Fay. Suddenly the steel-grey horse, Charon, pricked forward his ears gazing westward up the ridge.

Tedro gave one look, vaulted to his saddle and sent the horse pell-mell down along the ridge eastward. Four riders had broken from the timber. Spread out abreast, they were dashing after Tedro and the fading twilight glinted on the blued steel of drawn six-shooters. One against four in the open the cowboy hadn't a show of fighting it out. As he bent forward riding for his life, the drumming thud of hoofs was smothered by the crashing roar of guns. Bullets bit rocks and soil behind Tedro, to his right and left.

The killers were well mounted. Perhaps he'd out-ride them. Perhaps he wouldn't. He fished a sheet of paper from his vest pocket—his message to Ike—tore it and Ike's note to him and Foreman Jess Walker's letter to tiny scraps which fluttered along in the wake of his desperately racing horse.

A glance to the rear told him that one man had pulled up at the lone pine. He was loading the cash on his mount. The other three were losing ground; their six-shooters useless at this range. In another minute Tedro Ames would be into the woods—and safe! But even as this exultant thought flashed through his mind, from the edge of the timber towards which he sped, rang the spiteful crack of a rifle.

Tedro's horse, Charon, turned end over end crashing to earth in a cloud of dust and loosened stones. Hurled forward ahead of the falling horse the cowboy skidded along the ground, struck a rock head first and lay very still. The last he remembered for an indefinite time was hearing the rifle, seeing its flash and feeling his mount buckle and fold up under him.

When some indefinite time later he recovered consciousness, Tedro Ames discovered that he was securely tied to a saddle on a horse's back and going somewhere. Two men rode ahead of him; one behind. Gradually, as his aching head cleared he made out that all three were masked. Masked! This meant the fellows belonged to the Black Aces.

"Might be heaps worse," thought Tedro. "I'm still alive. Ain't that a miracle!" He thought of his activities following his escape from Truesdale at the H K ranch, and added: "Maybe it ain't no miracle. The boss Spade Ace wants to ask me a heap of questions and these jaspers know that."

Overhead were the stars. His gaze sought the big dipper, which told him it was only about nine o'clock, and the country across which the party was traveling was familiar. They were following up the valley of the

94

Swiftwater on the west side of it and—Tedro noted a landmark—were only three miles from the Swiftwater town.

"Takin' me there, so the snorty citizens can dangle me," he mused. "These Black Aces are full of lovely ideas." He concentrated upon studying the men's clothing, their horses, their saddles, the build of the men themselves. Masks might hide faces but there were other ways of identifying night riders. Abruptly one of the riders in the lead spoke, his voice muffled by his mask:

"I tell you again the stuff shore wasn't on Tedro, ner on Charon. 'Course he hid it, but the boss'll make him cough up."

"You bet," grunted the other and turned his head to look at Tedro, who instantly acted as if still unconscious. " 'Twould int'rest an' agitate Miss McKenzie powerful tuh know Ike Bowlaigs was stopped so they ain't no chance o' her coyboys comin' home."

The first speaker chuckled grimly. "Not a chance o' them punchers turnin' up 'til atter we're far along on our way to parts elsewhere."

Never had young Tedro Ames felt such a sense of shock. Ike, the peppery-tongued old range veteran whom Tedro loved had been stopped! And "stopped" more than likely meant shot dead.

Having read Foreman Jess Walker's letter to Fay, Tedro now realized that the Half Moon cowpunchers had been deliberately sent on a wild goose chase. This by means of a faked telegram, supposedly coming from Bill McKenzie. The cowboy recalled one line of Walker's letter: "Coupla yahoos bummed him (McKenzie) for passes and went along." Those yahoos, thought Tedro, had sent the telegram to Jess Walker. The tentacles of the octopus Black Aces reached far. Naturally those two fellows, dubbed yahoos by Jess and considered harmless by him, were of the dread organization. They were riding close herd on old Bill McKenzie, as he shipped cattle—for no honest purpose.

Tedro's scalp, a very sore scalp, and neck prickled with a sensation of cold horror. When Bill McKenzie marketed beef he always carried the cash received home with him. This time the chances were a hundred to one that an accident would happen to old Bill somewhere along the railroad on his homeward trip. After his body was discovered the cash would be noticeably missing of course. And Tedro Ames, probably the only fellow who had reasoned this out, was a prisoner on his way to where? Certainly not to talk to any sheriff or to any honest man. His captors were of the Black Ace brand.

The small party now turned to the right, splashed across a ford and halted on the farther bank while one man rode ahead to investigate in Swiftwater. Tedro's two remaining guards said nothing nor did he break the silence. What was the use? He had already found that not only were his hands tied snugly to the saddle horn, but his feet were so closely hobbled together under the horse's belly that he could not even kick the animal. It was a stolid plug anyhow which would have been overtaken in five jumps had the cowboy been able to make a break for freedom. He knew to whom it belonged. He had often seen it and the other horses ridden by these three men. In spite of their masks he also knew the men! But little good this was going to do him.

The third fellow returned. "Main Street's buzzin'," he announced. "But we can reach the hoosegow all jake."

Captors and prisoner circled to the north coming eventually to a silent and dark back street, where they drew up before a low, flat-roofed stone building. One man entered and came out immediately, jingling a bunch of keys.

"O.K.," he said.

The other two dragged Tedro from his saddle, without untying a cord which bound his wrists together, and boosted him into the jail. The barred door of a cell clanged shut behind him with a dismal note of finality.

Tedro heard horses going away. He lifted his hands to his mouth, found the knot in the cord on his wrists and worried it loose with his teeth. Then he rubbed his wrists and ankles, stretched and flexed his muscles. If only his head would stop aching. Rather strange that in all this mixup he had not lost his hat, the battered old black sombrero that had belonged to ill-fated Ab Thurston.

Soon steps sounded in Sheriff Potter's office and

Tedro stood well back in his cell gazing through slits in the barred door. Someone lighted the sheriff's lamp on his desk and in this yellow light Tedro saw lanky Jim Knowlton the postmaster, Ray Thomas, of the *Swiftwater Star,* Harmon Truesdale and a stranger. A neat chap this stranger in city clothes, square-jawed and sharp-eyed. The bulge of his coat indicated that he wore a heavy gun in a shoulder holster.

An odd contrast was Ray Thomas the fighting editor. Bareheaded as usual, his long uncombed hair flowed out from his head in every direction, a wild mop. He wore a black vest closely buttoned, splattered with ink, its pockets filled with pens and pencils. His trousers seemed about to slide off and his soiled shirt ballooned out above their waistband, while his collar, supposed to be white, was unbuttoned on one side; his tie up under his left ear. Spry, hatchet-faced and quick spoken, this was the editor of the *Swiftwater Star*, a character about town.

Truesdale wore a white bandage over his left eye. His right looked baleful and savage. Otherwise his features were as stonily composed as always. He said now:

"I didn't think Potter would be here. Doubt if he'll be in tonight, Marshal Ormsdale," looking at the stranger.

"Wa-al," vouchsafed Postmaster Jim with a nasal twang, "here four of us be and I cal'late we might talk things over right here. Quiet and we ain't like to be interrupted."

"Jim's right," said Thomas. "It's quiet here. Any place on Main Street folks'll butt in with their ears pinned back and eyes buggin'. Mr. Truesdale, I'm for givin' the U. S. Marshal, here, to investigate threats being sent through the mail, all the dope we can."

"Certainly," said Truesdale and sat down in the sheriff's chair. "How much have you told Ormsdale, Jim?"

"Everything I know," the postmaster replied.

"And a lot he guessed at," stated the Marshal drily. "Hank Farnum—that picturesque old stage driver and one of the biggest natural liars on earth—had a lot of theories, too. What we want to get at is facts. First—"

"Who's out there?" demanded Ray Thomas. Two horsemen had appeared in the lane of light streaming from the door and Tedro could see them—Jake Stoddard and the "long-geared, peanut-headed" Greasy Holderness. Tedro's eyebrows drew together and furrows formed between his eyes. They had changed clothes this pair and they no longer wore masks, nor did they ride the same horses, but Tedro knew that they—with Leonard M. Stoddard—*had brought him to this jail!*

"Oh, hello, boys," greeted Thomas from the open door. "Anything new?"

"Nope," said Holderness.

"Nope?" iterated Thomas. "You coming in?"

"Figgered maybe the sheriff'd be yere to give us more orders," said Holderness. "We'll wait out yere for him." He swung off and squatted on the ground holding his horse. Jake Stoddard followed suit.

"They'll wait all right!" thought Tedro. "Fella, you're in a bear trap with spiked jaws. How to get out?" He sets his wits to work.

Truesdale announced: "I'll tell the boys what to do," and went abruptly out, closing the door behind him.

Tedro regarded the three men who were left in the office, men who had no least idea he was there. Honest men all three, he thought, but could he make them believe his side of this grim and terrible business? Not a chance, he decided, and kept very still.

Thomas was addressing the marshal: "The latest news I have is that tonight, Saturday night, three ranchers are going to hand out cash to these damnable terrorists."

"Great Scott!" ejaculated Ormsdale. "Is no one setting a trap for—?"

"Uh-huh. The dope is—I got it confidential, but you and Jim are O.K.—that Sheriff Potter is trying for to grab some of the Black Aces. He's working at the I Dot Seven. And," Thomas lowered his voice, "Leonard Stoddard is s'posed to be setting a trap at the Pick Bar."

"That's good. Fine. This is different than working in a city, yet it seems to me that these crooks could be caught red-handed getting the money."

"About the aces sent through the mail—" Jim Knowlton began.

"One of our saloon men," said Thomas almost whispering, "W. Rawley, got his orders. He's his own

100

banker. The skunks seem to know everybody's business. They told him to dig up fourteen thousand dollars. He told me that was every cent he had in cash."

"Eh? Is this Rawley going to—?" the Marshal began.

Thomas nodded, his hair flying. "Rawley's paying them."

Ormsdale ripped out an oath. "A hellish state of affairs when men yield to extortionists without—"

"Three men have been shot on this range," said Thomas significantly. "And two of 'em are very dead. Carter's still alive, but he may not live long."

The Marshal changed color. "Who are they—these Black Aces?"

In the dark cell Tedro's lips formed words: "I can name some of 'em for you. But I won't just yet."

"We don't know!" cried the postmaster. "Tedro Ames is rumored to be one of 'em. But I don't believe it."

Tedro lifted his eyelids. "I won't forget that, Jim."

"Nor do I believe it," said Ray Thomas. "You see, Marshal, this Ames wasn't the kind of a fellow to go bronc. The laziest, easy-come, easy-go cowpuncher you ever saw. No thought for the morrow, nor a care, laughing at life and you'd laugh with him and like him."

Truesdale came quickly in and left the door open. From his one good eye a vindictive glance shot toward the unlighted cell where Tedro Ames sat on a cot, peering out between the bars. But the banker did not announce that a prisoner was present. Outside, the two men still squatted on the ground, smoking cigarettes, holding their horses—"humdingin' good horses" Tedro noted—and waiting. Waiting as Tedro knew for Ormsdale, Jim Knowlton and Thomas to go away. After which—

"How far you fellows got?" demanded Truesdale bruskly.

"Nowhere," said Ormsdale. "Jim, let's see those spade aces you have gathered; those with the writing on them, and several of the pink envelopes. If only we can find the man who wrote the threats. . . . Mr. Truesdale, are you an expert on handwriting? You should be and you should know more about the different signatures of residents here than anyone else."

"I do," the banker stated. "Already I have studied the penmanship on these threats with a magnifying glass; the addresses on the envelopes also. . . . I'm baffled. It's the clever work of a stranger, I'd say, Marshal."

"Here ye be, Marshal," spoke Jim. "I got three black aces and six pink envelopes."

"Ah. I have a first-class magnifying glass at my house, gentlemen," said Truesdale. "Perhaps you three would like to go there. Jim, you can take the marshal and Thomas up while I make a brief visit in this neighborhood. I'll be along shortly."

"Oh, ye-ah," thought Tedro.

"We'll do as you kindly suggest," the postmaster began. Then jumped in the air and spun around.

"What be that noise?"

A hollow groan had sounded; a groan as of someone in agony.

"Comes from that cell!" ejaculated the Marshal.

"Sure does!" Thus Ray Thomas as he snatched the keys off the desk. "Has Potter got a prisoner?" He was unlocking the cell.

Tedro saw Truesdale gnash his teeth. In a second the banker's face was composed again, but in that instant he had shown his black rage. Jake Stoddard and Greasy Holderness had left their horses and reached the outer door. They stood one on either side of it, looking into the office, while their saddlers, bridle reins a-trail, promptly trotted away into the night. This to Tedro's dismayed chagrin. His cell door now snapped open, but the cowboy, far from being discovered alert and on his feet, lay doubled up on the cot, moaning hollowly.

"This bird's powerful sick," clipped Ray Thomas. "Give me a hand. We'll carry him out and see what's wrong."

The marshal took one end of the cot, Thomas the other. They set it down in the center of the office. Lanky Jim Knowlton was holding the lamp for a better light. He trembled with excitement.

"Why, it be Tedro Ames!"

"Look, his hands are tied," spoke Truesdale. "Just coming back to his senses or something."

"Wonder who put him in there?" gasped Thomas. "Boy! What a story for my paper!"

"Men," Truesdale commanded, "I'll stay here with him. One of you get a doctor and one get a—uh—a bottle of whisky. The other get hot water and cloths. Lots of both. We want to save this fellow, so he can talk."

"O.K.," cried Thomas. "Come—"

" 'Twon't be necessary!" boomed Tedro Ames. He was off the cot. He had kicked the lamp from Jim's shaking hands. Crash of broken glass. Inky darkness. A lurid oath from the dignified banker of Swiftwater. A human form darting through the door and as it passed the two men there, men clawing at their holstered guns—a right fist smashed to the face of one; a left to the stomach of the other.

Holderness folded up in the middle. Jake Stoddard measured his length on the earth. Harmon Truesdale leaped through the door with his gun blazing. Blazing at a human figure vanishing around one corner of the jail. The next moment pandemonium was breaking loose on Main Street, while Ray Thomas, crowding out past Truesdale, was yelling, "Out of my way. Must get to my sanctum and write this up. 'Nother extra. Man! What a story!"

"Damn you, and your stories!" barked Truesdale venomously—as if the editor was to blame.

CHAPTER SEVEN
BANDITS THREE

On this bright Sunday morning Fay McKenzie's face looked wan and drawn; her pretty blue eyes, usually so bright and sparkling showed the effects of a sleepless, shuddery night. A shuddery night indeed, for Fay had known mental upset little short of torture. A shattering, killing blow had been dealt her faith in Tedro Ames. Yet her intuition had warred with cold logic and reason all the night long.

The evidence of her senses—for there was no denying the witness of her own eyes—told her that Tedro had appeared at the lone pine to get the cash demanded by the Black Aces. Intuition cried out that Tedro could never have fallen so low. What if he had loped directly to the rendezvous, swung off and picked up the sack of money? He could explain it. Last night instead of becoming panicked and racing madly for home she should have ridden to the man and demanded the truth.

The girl had been almost a mile from Wind Ridge when she heard the crashing of six-shooters, making the early darkness hideous with their death music. She had reined up, filled with curiosity and fear; wanting to gallop back to the lone pine and see what the shooting portended, yet not daring to do so. If a posse or a bunch of enraged ranchers had caught Tedro making off with the money and opened fire on him that was as it should be. No, it wasn't. It wasn't! Yes, it was.

The rattling gunfire had died away, followed by nothing but silence from Wind Ridge and Fay had ridden on home. Once during the night she had gotten out of bed, dressed and resolved to attempt to find out something about that fight. But in the dark what could she see or do alone? She had not gone. However it was now morning, breakfast over, the sun on the job, the ranch hands, the blacksmith and the cook at work, and Fay was saddling Torchy—to lope out to Wind Ridge.

Afterwards she would go to Swiftwater for news. There would be no stage today, for it was Sunday, and how she would miss Hank Farnum's gossip, the mail, in this land where there were, as yet, no telephones. Ike Bowlaigs should be home not later than this evening to report Bill McKenzie's answer to his telegram, and Fay hoped the cowboys would be with Ike. The Half Moon—every honest cow outfit and the citizens of Swiftwater—needed Jess Walker and his fighting crew to help round up the Black Aces. One thing was settled now and a tremendous weight off her mind; she had paid the extortionists and her father's life was safe. Safe.

The girl really had nothing to worry about now— except how in the world she was going to pay Banker Truesdale sixteen thousand dollars she had borrowed; make good also four thousand dollars of her father's money she had used. And how in the world was she going to explain to that stern, tight-fisted man, her father who was every bit as obstinate as Frank Carter, why she had considered it absolutely necessary to raise the cash? He'd swear his pet Scotch oath and snort:

"Lass, I dinna think I'd see the day when anybody'd bluff a McKenzie. Ye should ha' called their bluff. Gaing to shoot me? Ridiculous, when I was riding the train hundreds of miles away."

Oh, McKenzie thought the world and all of his bonny daughter, but he'd explode about that money. She feared he would never forgive her. But she had done right—the only thing she could do, yet it was Tedro who had taken that cash.

She could not get him out of her mind, recalling unforgetable days of long ago. Not so very long ago, though they seemed remote and distant now. The carefree, boyish lover, before he had inherited his uncle's T A ranch, penniless, working for Frank Carter, riding snorty broncs to call on Fay in the twilight; taking her out in the starlight along the dim mountain trails. Once a dun bronc had suddenly "come undone" on a steep sidehill, bucking like mad, plunging over a bank into a bog hole, and when Fay had dared to look, her heart in her throat, there was Tedro astride the bronc, mired half way up its sides in mud. Entirely unruffled, he had glanced around and grinned at her, lifted his hat, scratched his curly black head and drawled: "We seem to have stopped. But maybe this ol' cow can waller his way out."

A driving rain storm, lightning vivid and terrifying, crashing thunder rolling along the mountains; Fay caught without her slicker seeking shelter at the Circle C line camp. Tedro Ames helping her from her wet saddle, carrying her inside his cabin, where a half dozen pans caught water that dripped through the roof he would not fix. Tedro building up a roaring fire in the rusty old stove, baking biscuits, frying trout, making coffee for her, and no meal had ever tasted quite so good. After that he had given her his slicker and taken her home, through the downpour, that soaked him to the skin. She had said:

"Tedro, it's a wild night and getting wilder. You'd better stay at the bunkhouse and—"

He had kissed her in the rain— In fancy she could still feel the beat of streaming water on her upturned face and the pressure of his lips. He had leaped to his saddle without touching stirrup and gone away singing: "Bring me back my saddle; bring me back my gun."

Unforgetable days along the trail of romance. Other incidents, too, all unforgetable. Moonlight, youth, dreams, love. But what of dreams and love now? If Tedro still cared he should have come to the Half Moon on the evening of the day when he prevented her being robbed, or on the following day. If he cared and had not actually gone to the wild bunch he would have come. Fay was forgetting that she had sent him away, telling him it was all over; forgetting also that he might well have reasoned that the Half Moon was being watched for him.

She tugged a latigo tight and led Torchy out of the stable into the sunshine, and there, riding through the gate into the yard was Leonard M. Stoddard. Stoddard the efficient, hardworking rancher. Nothing boyish or carefree or happy-go-lucky about this tall, iron-muscled and iron-faced fellow. Life to him was no glad sweet song, rather serious business, so grim and real that his leathery features seldom cracked with a smile; his eyes never lighted with a twinkle. Here was the personification of purpose in life and ambition contrasting sharply with Fay's romantic memories of Tedro who had never seemed to have either purpose or ambition.

Len Stoddard lifted his hat and bowed gallantly. "I told you I'd be calling and I've got a two-pound box of candy for the prettiest girl in—"

"Len, what's the news? I'm so glad to see somebody."

"Make that more specific. Glad to see me?"

"Even you," and the girl mustered a smile. "And thank you for the candy. But you've been leading a posse and perhaps you can tell me about the fight on Wind Ridge last night."

Little did the girl realize that she was talking to one of five men who had captured Tedro Ames last night, who had taken Tedro to the Swiftwater jail.

"Nothing," said Stoddard. "I wasn't in the vicinity. Was there a fight on Wind Ridge and what's your interest, Fay?" He regarded her intently.

"Then you know nothing about it?" She showed her disappointment. "I—well—Tedro—I heard guns talking."

"I see. What about Tedro?"

"Did I mention his name? Perhaps he's somewhat in my thoughts since he's become so—I mean such a famous horse trader."

Len Stoddard did not smile though the corners of his tight mouth quivered slightly. "I see you read the paper. I can tell you the latest news from town before Thomas' new extra reaches you. His glaring headline will be: 'TEDRO AMES ESCAPES COUNTY JAIL! WHO PUT AMES IN JAIL REMAINS A DEEP, DARK MYSTERY!'"

Fay merely looked at the man wide-eyed. He hunched his shoulders, resumed: "No, I don't know who could have put this wild man in jail. No one else seems to have the slightest idea, but Potter has not been heard from."

"How strange! How'd he escape?" Fay's heart was beating double-quick time. Deep down inside, she was glad, mighty glad that Tedro had won clear. Glad though this was a victory for intuition against reason and logic. Also she was, oh, so relieved to know he had not been killed in the fight on Wind Ridge!

"It'll be in the paper so can't you wait?" said Stoddard. Then: "Fay, why are you still interested in that fellow? He's no good. Furthermore—mind, I'm not saying so myself—they are saying in Swiftwater that undoubtedly he is one of the Black Aces, possibly the leader."

The girl bit her quivering lower lip. "Who's saying so?"

"Harmon Truesdale, and his word amounts to something."

"Umn? That doesn't prove it, however."

"Still sticking up for him, girl. I can't understand women."

"No, and I don't think you ever will. How'd Tedro escape?"

"Just the same I'd like to try to understand one woman. Give me a chance. Your father approves of me. I'm steady, a worker, doing pretty well; chances are I'll do even better. Fay, you wouldn't be making any mistake to—"

"How'd Tedro get away?"

"Tedro. Tedro!" Stoddard snapped his fingers irritably and his grim face set in harsh lines. "I try to make love to you and I hear nothing but inquiries about that fellow. . . . He got out by a trick."

With this the man related what had taken place at the jail. "If I'd been there it wouldn't have happened," he concluded.

"I'm glad you weren't there, Len. . . . Tedro smashed the lamp, knocked your brother, Jake, cold, doubled the peanut-headed Greasy Holderness up in a knot—real man stuff!"

Stoddard muttered something under his breath which sounded like an oath. "Fay McKenzie, you must know there are strong suspicions that the fellow murdered my foreman. You do know that he held you up and shot Arch Greenwald when Greenwald interfered and fled only because Sheriff Potter—"

"That's a lie and I'm going to face Potter and force him to tell the truth. Get it straight and tell it straight, Len. Arch Greenwald held me up, and fired at Tedro before ever Tedro shot him."

"Anyway, this fellow, Ames, is caught in a net from which he can't escape. . . . Fay, it's possible that I might forget my duty as a deputy sheriff, a posseman, and help him to get clear, leave the country, if—" Stoddard broke off.

"If?" asked Fay, though she had already guessed the answer.

"If you'll give me your promise to marry me when I tell you he's safely out?"

"Beautiful fall weather we're having," said Fay. "Yet I wish it would storm so we could find tracks in the snow—tracks left by these night-working coyotes. Any other news from town?"

After remaining silent for nearly a minute, perhaps to gain control of his voice and his temper, for his eyes betrayed his baffled rage, Stoddard returned steadily, "Yes, a snowstorm would help us lots. Other news? It's reported that Sheriff Potter's trap to catch the Black Aces at the I Dot Seven failed. No one showed up to collect. W. Rawley of the Oasis Saloon paid the scoundrels to the tune of fourteen thousand dollars. . . . Miss McKenzie, I myself have been threatened." He fished from his vest pocket one of the now familiar spade-ace cards, handed it to the girl.

"You Stoddard Brothers," Fay read: "Put eleven thousand dollars, cash, at Pinnacle rocks directly east of your ranch at eight o'clock Sunday night. Fail to do this and you will both be shot. Black Aces."

Fay caught her breath. "What are you going to do? Aren't you scared?"

"Scared? Me? Not a bit, nor they won't bluff us. Jake and I have cooked up a scheme. I won't tell even you what it is, but shortly after eight tonight there'll be at least one Black Ace less. I—we're not the men to take a gouge like that lyin' down. . . . Where were you going, Miss McKenzie?"

"I was going to town, but as you've told me the news I guess I'll stay home."

"And I must be joining my posse. Be seeing you again when—"

"Yes, join your posse and look for tracks on Wind Ridge. See what you can tell from them."

"Be seeing you again when I've rounded up a Black Ace—or the whole bunch. . . . Fay, doesn't it make any difference to you that I may be shot dead tonight?"

Fay looked away towards Flame Peaks glorious with the morning sunlight warring with cloud mists. "Oh, I don't want anybody to be shot. This is all terrible. But, Len, you said you weren't scared, had a plan to get the Black Aces' cash collector, and—and if you mean does my fear of your being shot make me love you, it doesn't. You're all right, but I just don't care for you that way. . . . Good-bye."

The girl turned and led Torchy into the stable. When she saw the man disappear along the road to Swiftwater without looking back, she whispered, "He isn't going out to Wind Ridge to run down tracks that must still be pretty warm. I'll just go myself. Can't stand sticking around the house anyhow."

Her eyes were sparkling once again. She'd be doing something to get a line on the terrorists. Why hadn't she done more before? Strange that news of Tedro's escape from jail should bring color back to her cheeks, and a surge of joy to her heart when she wasn't at all sure but what he really was one of the dread organization. She ran to tell her mother:

"I'm taking a ride out in the foothills to see if I can find any cattle."

Mrs. McKenzie thought that nothing unusual. Fay often rode alone. "Take Scottie with you," she advised, however.

And Scottie, the dark-haired reliable old collie, was romping joyfully ahead of Torchy as Fay rode south. The girl had, however, changed to her range-riding clothes. She now wore a slouchy, discolored old Stetson, a dark blue jumper over her soft gray shirt, overalls, boots and spurs. From a distance almost anyone would have taken her to be a youthful cowboy.

The first thing she saw as she reached the top of Wind Ridge were dozens of magpies and crows reluctantly taking wing as Scottie noisily interrupted their morning meal—the carcass of a horse. Three coyotes also slunk away to the timber looking back and licking their chops. Soon then, Fay discovered that the horse was Banker Truesdale's splendid mount, Charon.

The day was still, nor had the wind blown during the night. Therefore horse tracks on the ridge had not been obliterated. From her earliest recollections this range-raised girl had been taught by her father, Ike Bowlaïgs, old Henry Kline and others to read tracks and trail signs. She was no wizard at it, but she was better than the average cowhand. Therefore she correctly read the story of what had happened, but who could the men be that had captured the rollicky cowboy last night?

From tracks, the girl discovered that there had been five of these fellows, and they had had one extra horse. Tedro had been placed on this horse and three of the men had started to Swiftwater with their prisoner. The other two men had turned back towards the mountains. Angry and vexed that Len Stoddard had not seen fit to follow her suggestion of attempting to track these night riders, the girl set out to trail this pair herself. Tracks led her westward into the rough and wooded foothills. However, within a mile these tracks seemed to vanish mysteriously and she could not again find them, nor was old Scottie of any help.

"Well," the girl reasoned, "the men turned either north or south, because for a stretch forty miles long there is no pass over Flame Range. So I'll ride north."

Soon thereafter she reached a crossing on Trail Rest Creek at the base of the mountains, and at this crossing she found plain horse tracks.

No longer ago than yesterday evening four horses had forded this rushing little stream, headed southward. Two had crossed it a few hours later, at this same place headed northward. These tracks corresponded exactly with those of two of the animals which pointed south. As Fay read the sign, four of the five men who had clashed with Tedro on Wind Ridge had come from the north; two had returned along this same route—not following any trail, just cutting across the rough hills and deep valleys adjacent to the towering mountains.

All excitement and anticipation the girl did likewise. She lost the tracks and found them again by keeping onward to the north in almost a direct line. She dipped down into deep canyons and climbed out of them; Torchy ascending the steep, steep slopes by zigzagging back and forth. Slow, hard traveling, mile after mile, always to the north.

When at last she paused a-top a ridge where a cold wind sweeping down from Flame Peaks chilled Fay to her very bones, the sun was dipping low to the west, the day almost spent. Yet she had not found from where those fellows had come; to what place two of them returned. But here on this ridge was a trail beaten out by horse hoofs; a trail which she had never before seen and had not known existed. Undoubtedly, if one followed it eastward it led to Swiftwater Valley; if one rode west on up the ridge where would it lead? Apparently to the two hoary Flame Peaks themselves.

Impossible, Fay thought, and yet horse tracks told her the four men had come from the mountains; two had returned by the same route. Fay McKenzie, known as Sandy, whispered exultantly: "I do believe I've found the outlaw trail!"

Scottie, the faithful collie who had followed her, and sometimes led her all this day, lay down in front of Torchy with his red tongue hanging out and his friendly eyes saying: "Well, what next, lady?" and Fay answered:

"The thing for us to do, old fellow, is get out of here, find somebody we know we can trust and tell him about this. Um, maybe Jess and the punchers'll be home this evening."

She swung from her saddle, sat on a small boulder and patted Scottie's head when he placed it on her knee. "Yes, you smart old cow dog, that's the wisest thing for us to do, and the safest. But wouldn't you like to follow this trail up toward Flame Peaks and see where it leads, where it ends? I would. I'd do it, too, if only someone—Tedro was with me. . . . What was that?"

Scottie pricked forward ears pointed up the ridge which curved so that by no means its entire length was in sight of the girl, her dog and her horse.

Again came the sound. This time it was unmistakable—the metallic ring of iron-shod hoofs striking rocks. Fay was on her feet startled and afraid for the first time this day. What to do? If this was the outlaws' trail, and she, a woman alone, was discovered—

"Now don't you bark, Scottie," she whispered. "Not a sound out of you. We must hide."

Scottie wagged his tail, cocked his head to one side and very plainly said that he understood. Yonder at the rim of the ridge the timber began, a heavy growth of pines on the steep side hill. Quickly Fay led Torchy into these, Scottie right at her heels. She had no fear that the intelligent dog would betray their presence.

The ring of steel shoes on rocks was much closer. The girl held her hand on Torchy's nostrils and was glad that the pony was tired and indifferent. She peered out through the branches. Three riders were passing, one astride a pinto horse upon which Fay's eyes riveted. It was the pinto Apache. Something sinister about the tall, swarthy and hook-nosed rider. He carried a scabbarded rifle. So did his companions, a young fellow, not much larger than the girl herself, and a stocky, bull-necked man with brutal face half hidden by black whisker stubble.

This individual fitted Fay's ideas of a first-class brigand—a killer. His mount, a stocking-legged bay with a blazed face, was the same horse Fay had seen Tedro riding the day she had been held up—outlaw Wolf Whalen's horse. Seeing these two horses now,

118

the pinto and the bay, doubts concerning Tedro again assailed the girl, for she knew nothing of Tedro's having traded with Wolf Whalen.

The youngest outlaw was speaking and she listened with all her ears: "Ain't we kinda careless, ridin' this-a-way, Chief? In daylight and on a ridge."

"Yeh," admitted Wolf Whalen. "But there ain't nawthin' much to fear 'til ranchers get organized proper and we'll know well ahead o' time when that happens."

" 'Twon't be 'til the Half Moon rannies get home," offered the brutal-faced man. "Jess Walker an' his crew is the most 'ficient jaspers in this neck the woods an' the only ones we're scart o'."

Wolf Whalen voiced a sort of satanic chuckle: "And they got sent on a wil' goose chase, so they won't be back 'til we're all through and a-hittin' the trail."

Fay barely caught this for the outlaws were going on down country. Her eyes flashed: "You've got another guess coming, Mister Outlaw," she whispered fiercely. "For once little Sandy McKenzie's hunch was right. She saw through that fake telegram to Jess, and the Half Moon cowboys'll be on the job before you know it!"

The three had vanished behind timber farther down the ridge. Fay scratched Scottie's ears: "We know more than we did, old faithful. Now where are those scoundrels going and what hellishness are they up to tonight? I want to follow 'em, find out. But you, Scottie, get this, are to go home."

119

Scottie looked hurt. "It's very necessary. You're to take a message to the ranch and get there as soon as you can. You understand? Home—with a message?"

Scottie started away. Fay called him back. "You old dear, if the stupid sheriff had your sense this outlaw crew—they're the Black Aces or at least a part of that terrible gang of thieves and killers—would have been rounded up long ago. . . . No, wait, Scottie, 'til I write a note, and I'll put it in my glove and tie my glove to your collar. When you get there, you must make the folks understand."

Ten minutes later Scottie, the dark-haired reliable old collie, was loping with the peculiar sideways single-foot of the dog or the wolf across country air line for the Half Moon ranch. The evening star was just peeping out, and Fay McKenzie thrilled to the danger and excitement as she stealthily trailed three outlaws. Certainly this was no place for any girl, no job for any girl, but, if luck rode with her, before the night was ended she'd lead Jess Walker and the Half Moon cowboys to Wolf Whalen's lair. So she thought *little knowing that Ike Bowlaigs had never reached Harpoon!*

CHAPTER EIGHT
MOST DANGEROUS MAN

Tedro Ames lay flat on the roof of the Swiftwater jail watching lanterns bob here, there, everywhere about the town as groups of men sought him. He had circled and come back to the jail within five minutes after his escape and had climbed to the roof before Truesdale and others had left. Therefore he had been in time to hear the banker, in a voice choked with blind rage, say:

"Spread the word. Ames is to be shot at sight like you'd shoot a wolf. Undoubtedly he's a Black Ace and I believe, the leader of the extortionist mob. The most dangerous man in Swiftwater Valley. Kill him at all costs."

"Partly right, Mister Truesdale," thought the cowboy. "It happens I am the most dangerous man in Swiftwater Valley—to you and *your extortionist mob. Not mine. Yours!*"

And wasn't it ironical that Tedro was caught in such a strange web of circumstances that he could not, dared not, go openly to the citizens and tell them the truth? Tell them that he knew Harmon H. Truesdale was the brains and the leader of the Black Aces, that he knew five others of the pack—Leonard and Jake Stoddard, Greasy Holderness, Boyd Loomis, the hardware merchant, and Mooch, the bar-fly.

Who among the honest and reliable citizens would credit such an astounding accusation? No one. Especially when it came from a fugitive cowpuncher accused of murder, accused himself of being a Black Ace; the cowpuncher whom Truesdale had announced must be shot at sight. Truesdale himself, the Stoddards, and doubtless all others of the dread organization would like very very much to put a rifle bullet through this troublesome cowboy. To them dynamite was milk and crackers compared to the hitherto easy-going, peaceful, irresponsible, Tedro Ames.

Being the kind of fellow he was, Tedro grinned while thinking of all this. Grinned and whispered: "Doubt if Truesdale sleeps a-tall t'night. He's like the feller who grabbed the wolf by the tail. I'm the wolf and he can't rest ner let go 'til that wolf's kilt."

He watched riders dash out of town in all directions to comb the nearby country; watched the bobbing lanterns throw grotesque shadows of men prowling the streets, looking into all buildings and alleys. But those searchers never came near the jail. Naturally it was the last place they'd think of looking. Gradually the tumult and excitement died and save for a few lanes of light from saloons which stayed open cutting patterns on Main Street the town became dark and silent.

Not until then did the fugitive stir, though he had been on tenterhooks for three hours. Dropping from the low roof he went directly to a tumbledown shack on the outskirts of Swiftwater. Behind the shack lay a makeshift corral and in this was a horse. As Tedro caught and saddled the animal, he chuckled: "Our most notorious horse trader."

He took a careful survey about the vicinity, then with a lariat in hand entered the shack without knocking. Mooch, the bar-fly, lifted his torso from his tattered quilts and Tedro, without one word, landed his right fist squarely on the fellow's chin. Such power behind this wallop that Mooch wilted without a sound. Tedro tied the man, wadded his clothes into a bundle, and found a gun which he belted on. He carried out the bundle and tied it behind the saddle. Mooch came next. Tedro threw him across the horse's withers, mounted and left town.

He was splashing across the river when a sentry hailed him from the farther bank. "Who rides?"

"Daggone! And there're two of 'em," thought Tedro, seeing the men and the dim outlines of horses behind them indistinctly. Naturally, it followed that they could see him only dimly. Instantly he turned his horse downstream in the breast-deep current, and as he did so he rolled out of his saddle, dragging Mooch with him into the ice-cold water.

"Headin' down stream!" clipped one man on the bank. "Hidin' on far side of his hoss!"

Holding to his helpless prisoner, Tedro dived, swam towards the shore. This was not the usual ford and the bank here was steep, rising a couple of feet above the water's edge. Tedro came up under its protection, heard the thump of boots and ring of spurs. The two guards were running downstream, one shouting:

"We'd better shoot the hoss. Make sure o' grabbin' the geezer whoever he is!"

"Not yet, Fred. Figger we can catch 'im alive."

"But that wallerin' hoss is makin' good time. We had ought to ha' hit our saddles. You figger it's Tedro?"

"Mebbe! You go back; get our broncs. I'll keep him in sight. Shoot if I have to."

Tedro had boosted Mooch out on the bank, climbed out himself. Two saddled horses were near at hand. One sentry was fully fifty yards away, but the other was returning as fast as he could run. Tedro dragged his prisoner behind a small bush, crouched low himself. The sentry arrived, jerked loose two pairs of bridle reins tied to a small alder. He was about to swing to his saddle when a dark figure rose behind him, grabbed him by the neck and the seat of his overalls and tossed him ungently far out into the river.

Glug! A wild yell was cut off short as the icy current caught the man and swept him downstream. Tedro Ames threw Mooch across one saddle, leaped to the other himself, and holding his captive with one hand guided his new mount with the other. They were gone, two horses and two men. But the sentry in the river had seen only one and that one far from clearly.

Downstream a voice was yammering: "What the blazes?"

But Tedro was not lingering to answer questions. Three hundred yards distant he pulled up and discovering slickers behind both saddles, put one on himself, threw the other around Mooch. The bar-fly had regained consciousness, was able to ride straight up, so Tedro, hobbling his feet from stirrup to stirrup, remarked:

"You was needin' a bath, Mooch, but this time o' year it shore gives a feller a bad case of teeth chatter. Le's ride and warm up."

Behind he heard a man swearing and another one yell: "Now we're afoot! That geezer got our nags and the darned hoss he was ridin' turned back toward town."

"Why didn't you—?"

"And why didn't you—" snarled the other. Then both men swore. Tedro fogging across country, said: "A couple of square citizens, sure as I'm all wet. I know their voices. Glad I didn't have to shoot 'em."

An hour later, he circled cautiously around the dark buildings at the H K ranch, then rode into the yard. "Kline," he called softly.

Old Henry Kline descended the ladder from his hay loft where he had been hiding and watching his house and the surrounding area. There was a rifle in his gnarled hands as he came out into the yard: "You catch one, Tedro? Who?"

"I got Mooch. Who'd you get—?"

"I tied onto our friend Boyd Loomis. No need o' goin' into details, but I got 'im afore dark. Got him locked in my dugout cellar behint the shack. Gosh, it's nigh midnight, Tedro. Whar you been?"

Tedro shrugged. His slicker rustled as he stepped from his saddle. "I was detained and I took a bath, and—"

"Wastin' time foolin' 'round takin' a bath times like this!" snorted the veteran rancher. "S'pose you shaved, too. This clenity's a kinder mania with you."

"Some say it's a good habit. Ain't I entitled to one good habit, Henry? . . . Get any dope outa Loomis?"

"Not a blat. Swars he doan know nothin', that he ain't one of 'em. But this bedbug you got here'll squeal. . . . Been swappin' hosses again, Tedro? 'Course I told you to get rid of Charon, 'cause anybody sightin' that hoss'd know you was ridin' him. . . . What'd you larn from Ike Bowlaigs? Don't s'pose you dared ride into the Half Moon to see the girl?"

"Henry, I told you how 'twas atween me and Sandy. She don't want to see me no more. If I'd allowed she wanted to see me, I'd ha' rid to the Half Moon, regardless of your idea that it's one of the ranches bein' watched for me to show up. . . . Let's take Mooch in and get inside ourselves. I'll get the 'monia 'less I get some dry duds pronto. Furthermore I got heaps to tell you and a job for you immejit."

They carried Mooch through the log cabin to the dugout at its rear. Tedro untied the fellow's hands and Kline gave him a couple of blankets to keep him warm. "The jigger's in his underclothes," he remarked. "Where's his clothes?"

"I left 'em tied to his saddle on his own hoss," Tedro informed. "How you feelin', Loomis?" to the man already in the dugout.

"I'll have the law on you scoundrels for this," rasped the hardware man of Swiftwater.

"Truesdale's law?" asked the cowpuncher. "He's to the end of his rope, Loomis. You'd jus' as well turn State's evidence, tell us the pass word, name every Black Ace, tell us where they all hang out."

"I'll see you in hell—" Loomis began.

"No doubt," said Tedro cheerfully. "You're headed that way on greased skids." He went out and closed the stout door, fastening it with an iron bar.

Kline blanketed the windows of his bachelor kitchen-living room before he lighted a lamp. "Can't tell who might be coyotin' around," he opined. "Gives me a queer feelin' like old times when Injuns was on the war path. . . . You reckon these Black Aces suspect I know anything 'bout 'em, Tedro?"

Tedro was changing his wet garments for some of the rancher's dry apparel. "Don't think so, Henry. You staged it plumb realistic, bangin' away at me that night I ran out on Truesdale's hoss."

"Figgered to make Truesdale and Loomis and Mooch think I was agin you," said Kline. "Told 'em some lies immejitly after you rambled, allowed you'd gone to the wild bunch proper, said I'd drill you at sight. But after they had gone back to town ridin' on my hosses you come danglin' in 'bout three o'clock."

"And we had a humdingin' breakfast I was needin' bad," grinned Tedro. "I'm a heck of a lookin' cowboy now, Ab Thurston's ol' black hat, your doggoned ragged clothes and warped boots any cowpuncher'd be ashamed to be caught dead wearin'. And I used to be a right natty dresser. . . . Kline, who can we trust—a cowpuncher?"

"The Half Moon rannies. Any one of Frank Carter's punchers."

"It's to get the Half Moon rannies that I want somebody to ride like the devil was after him to Harpoon and when he gets there he's to send some telegrams I'll now write."

"Why's this necessary?" demanded Kline, handing Tedro a tablet and pencil.

"We've got to get help. The Half Moon boys are the fellows we need. Ike Bowlaigs was stopped from reaching Harpoon yesterday. I s'pose he's dead." Rage suddenly filled Tedro's calm voice. "Just another of the reasons why I had to get out of that jail. A few more reasons bein' that the sonovaguns have robbed Sandy of I don't know how much, also I figger they aim to kill and rob her father, and because, outside of you, Henry, I'm the only man that even suspects who the curs actually are."

"Fate dealt you a hand you got to play out," said Kline. "You been in jail? How'd you get out?"

But Tedro, busy writing, replied tersely, "So saddle your hoss. You're to lope to the Circle C and get Slim Shafter on the job, pronto."

Ten minutes later Henry Kline was on his way to the Circle C, Frank Carter's ranch. He took with him two telegrams written by Tedro and signed "Sandy," because as Tedro explained both Bill McKenzie and Jess Walker would pay attention to a message from the daughter of the Half Moon where they'd pay little heed to one from Tedro Ames. Kline had specific verbal instructions to Slim Shafter, and the old rancher took with him the two horses which had just carried Tedro and Mooch to the H K. He was to turn them loose somewhere in the hills.

Immediately Kline was gone on his mission, Tedro cooked and ate an enormous meal. He remarked to nothing in particular: "I must be on a diet. One square about every twenty-four hours. . . . Can't kick so long as I get that good a break. As for sleep—I ought to have stored up enough in the past year since I became a rancher—and gentleman of leisure so I allowed—to last me through this deal."

He shoved back his chair and smoked a reflective cigarette thinking of Fay. Always his thoughts strayed to the bonny girl, all the more desirable and adorable because he now considered her unattainable. How pretty she had been with heightened color that day which seemed a year ago—so much had happened since —when she had told him he was through—a fool. But Ike Bowlaigs had said— Aw, well, Ike was talkin' through his hat. He had done it to keep Tedro off the outlaw trail. Good old Ike. Tedro was glad he hadn't taken that turn.

Had Fate decreed that he must play his hand in this drastic game of extortion and sudden death from the dark? A game the like of which had never before been known on the range where rustlers stole cattle and horses and outlaws robbed and went their way without ever resorting to such subtle and altogether terrible tactics as these Black Aces employed.

Well Tedro was in the deal clear to his ears and somewhat to his own amazement, when he had always been one to dodge and avoid trouble, he now found that he yearned to play out this hand, save and protect the ranchers and others yet to be robbed by the extortionists; avenge those who'd been wantonly murdered, restore to those already robbed their money and above all, pin the dead wood on the Black Aces, round them up and exterminate them—if necessary.

But, as he realized, he was working under terrific handicaps. False reports had damned him in the eyes of so many ranchers and citizens of Swiftwater that he knew not to whom he might appeal for help now. At present he had, since Ike's disappearance, only Henry Kline on his side. Tedro himself had not dared ride to the Circle C, to get Slim to go on the mission to Harpoon. Though Tedro had known Carter and his wife and his cowboys for years, he considered it most likely that they would attempt to take him a prisoner, refusing to believe anything he might tell them. But Kline could and would do what Tedro himself could not at the Circle C.

How to manage the situation now? Abruptly his

musings ceased. From without had sounded the thumpity-thump of a horse's hoofs. It could not be Kline, for he had not had time to reach the Circle C and return. 'Twas somebody else and here was Tedro inside the bachelor dwelling, lacking time even to reach the stable across the yard.

Swiftly he inspected his new gun—the one taken from Mooch—then blew out the lamp and waited in the dark room. Since the windows had been blanketed the newcomer—there was only one Tedro decided—would not know the place had been lighted. The horseman stopped in front of the house, swung off and rapped loudly. Very sleepily Tedro called:

"Come in."

The door swung wide and on the threshold Tedro saw by starlight Sheriff Pete Potter: "Hi, Kline?" called the sheriff.

"Ye-ah," grunted Tedro from the darkness. "What's on your mind?"

"I got word, 'bout midnight, from Truesdale. From Truesdale, mind you. He's taking charge of this hunt fer them Black Aces hisself. Got word to be lookin' fer Tedro Ames, special and partic'lar. So me and my posse has split up and are ridin' to ranches to warn everybody that bad egg's to be shot at sight."

"Glad you warned me," said Tedro. "Who knows you rid to the H K?"

"Hey?" rumbled the sheriff, startled. "Your voice! You ain't Henry Kline. Who—?" He reached for his Colt.

131

A streak of flame lanced out of the dark cabin which rocked to a thunderous explosion as a bullet ripped the holster from Potter's hip.

"I'm shot!" he gasped. "Don't—don't kill me."

"I won't, 'less you make it necessary. Come in, Sheriff. . . . Face the wall and poke your hands behint you, so. . . . No more guns on you? . . . That's jake. I'll take your belt. Now set in that chair and don't wiggle while I light up."

As lamplight once again flooded the cabin the sheriff, with wrists tied behind his back, stared saucer-eyed at his captor. "You, Tedro! The man I'm huntin'—here!"

"Uh-huh, and maybe a kind Santa Claus sent you, so I can put you wise to yourself. You're the law in Swiftwater Valley and you got a chance to cover yourself with glory. Tell me, Potter, is that thing above your shoulders solid bone?"

"You mean my head?"

"Correct the first guess. You're smarter'n I allowed." Tedro sat down across the little table from the officer and glared fiercely into his eyes. "Potter, why the devil did you make up that dirty lie 'bout me stickin' up Fay McKenzie and Greenwald gettin' shot 'cause he butted in?"

" 'Twasn't no lie. 'Twas the way I read the evidence. The gal tried to stand up for you, but she couldn't pull no wool over my eyes."

"Sandy told you the truth then?" Tedro felt a bit light-headed. For a doubt that had been tormenting his mind was removed. She had stuck up for him!

"Naw, not the truth," snorted the sheriff. "Folks knows how things was and still is, I guess, with you and Miz McKenzie. I tol' her straight she was lyin' fer you."

"Sheriff," said the cowpuncher, "I wish I knew whether you're just a plain dumb chump or one of the Black Aces."

"Me, one o' them killers!" Potter drew himself up affronted. "I'll have you know I'm an officer of the law, sworn to—"

"Do your duty," Tedro cut in. "O.K. Here's your chance to get a swelligant writeup in Ray Thomas' paper about— How's this for a headline? 'Pete Potter, our valorous sheriff, wipes out the Black Aces!'"

Potter nodded twice: "If I can get loose from you, maybe a splurge like that'll be in the *Swiftwater Star* some day. But s'long as my hands is tied and you got me what chance—?"

"Listen, bone-head, I'm goin' to give you a couple of earfuls of evidence and proof. Then you can go ahead and make history in this valley. Now, pay 'tention." Briefly Tedro related how last night he had arrived at the H K ranch; how he and Kline had been held up by four masked men, tied and later rescued by Truesdale, Boyd Loomis and Mooch, the bar-fly.

"They allowed they must take me to town, so Henry Kline offers 'em a hoss for me to fork," he concluded. "At Henry's stable, I all t'oncet go away from there with all of their nags. That's how come Banker Truesdale to have a black eye, also how come he offered a thousand bucks for Tedro Ames and spread the word I was now ridin' his steel-grey, Charon."

"You still forkin' Charon?" asked the sheriff.

"You're heaps behind on up-to-date news, Pete. Continuin' the story, I drop back to the H K 'bout three A.M. Like I figger may be the case, Henry Kline's tickled to see me. . . . I knew he would be when all the hot lead he threw after me went wild— and Henry a dead shot. . . .

"We put our heads together and at first crack of day we're out scoutin' for tracks. Now here's the story we read from tracks, Mister Sheriff. The four masked jiggers hid their hosses a little ways from where Kline was to put his cash for the Black Aces. The geezers themselves hid in the sagebrush on the hill, and because I was with Kline they stuck us up. If he'd been alone they'd ha' let him place his money.

"Three went back to their broncs and the one who stole my hoss joined 'em. He led the hoss he had been usin' and headed west into the mountains. The other three fiddled around for a little bit, then came and rescued me and Henry Kline. *Them three was Truesdale, Loomis and Mooch.* You get the significance, Sheriff?"

Sheriff Pete Potter merely looked blank. Tedro resumed, leaning forward across the table in his earnestness. "I upset their idea of takin' me to town by tannin' out on Truesdale's own hoss. Tied behind his saddle was his coat, rolled up in it a heavy canvas sack of money. When I got back to this H K ranch I showed this to Kline. It was the same canvas sack and the same identical money—he'd looked at the bills and the gold close—that he'd been robbed of!"

"If that's true," said the sheriff in a tone that showed his disbelief, "where's the dough?"

"None of your business," retorted the cowpuncher. He had given the money to Henry Kline, naturally, and he did not know what the rancher had done with it.

"Since you can't show that jack," Potter began, but Tedro interrupted:

"Not a doubt but that Truesdale, Loomis and Mooch belong to this hellish extortionist organization. Yes, and I got plenty more proof tonight that Truesdale, the leadin' citizen of Swiftwater, the honorable mayor and banker who nobody suspects, is the big boss bull of the Black Ace herd.

"Uh-huh, if it hadn't been he yearned to ask me plenty questions—and had so instructed his men— questions such as what I did with ten thousand dollars I found on his saddle, and what conclusions I drew from findin' it, and who I'd told—I'd ha' been layin' on Wind Ridge now, looking up at the stars with the wise coyotes payin' no attention to me, knowin' I was good and dead.

"And if it hadn't been that Ray Thomas, Postmaster Jim and the U. S. Marshal was at the jail this evenin' Tedro Ames wouldn't be talkin' to you now, Sheriff. Five men downed me t'night, early. Three of the five

I can name, Len and Jake Stoddard and Greasy Holderness. They're all Black Aces."

Again the cowpuncher stopped and Sheriff Potter looked at him very queerly. "It's shore some story, feller."

Tedro's eyes flashed, yet holding on to his temper he said calmly, "Just one thing more to prove and cinch all I've been tellin' you." He rose and took from the shelf above the stove Kline's coffee can. In this he and Henry Kline had hidden a certain sheet of paper which Tedro had found in Harmon Truesdale's coat pocket. Tedro had examined this before, but he now read the typewritten notations to the sheriff:

"The Half Moon. . . . $20,000, plus an equal amount—plus $25,000 or more.

W. Rawley. 14,000
Circle C. 12,000
H K 10,000
I Dot 7. 6,000
Pick Bar 7,000
T A 3,000
Elmswood . . . . 500"

There were a dozen more entries each naming an individual or a brand with varying amounts of money opposite the name or brand. The grand total of all the sums was one hundred and ninety thousand dollars.

"If this list was to come to light and Truesdale was asked what it meant," Tedro resumed, "he'd say, 'Anticipatin' the demands of the Black Aces I figured how much I could furnish each man—to save his life.' But it's mighty noticeable that Len Stoddard and his brother ain't on the list, nor Boyd Loomis, nor Greasy Holderness.

"Also it's powerful significant that Frank Carter was asked for an even twelve thousand bucks; Henry Kline for ten. I see I was down for three thousand— about every nickel my layout was worth. Evidently Fay McKenzie was asked for twenty thousand. The snakes got it, too. It also looks as if they intended to bleed the Half Moon for another twenty thousand, also, as I figure, rob old Bill of the cash he'll get for the shipment of beef he's now marketing.

"So you see this list is an estimate of how much the mob aims to clean up by its hellish scheme, and, as I get it," Tedro scratched the whisker stubble on his chin and thought he ought to shave, "accordin' to the plan, Mister Truesdale, the great benefactor and man who saves ranchers' lives in this shocking crisis by advancing them money, will be holdin' from fifteen to twenty first-mortgages (can't get his hooks into a few men who have actually got cash) when all the smoke and fire has died away.

"Truesdale, unsuspected of course of any remote connection with the Black Aces, will then remind the Circle C, the H K, the Pick Bar and others how he now expects the mortgages and interest to be taken up. Ye-ah, he has paid out his money and though he regrets the circumstances he must ask for its return."

Tedro's usually mild eyes were smoldering as he stared at the sheriff. But his voice did not lift as he resumed: "The slick hound. He and his mob will split the big wad they get, his helpers gettin' well paid. Then Truesdale aims to collect again. Talk about eatin' your cake and havin' it too!"

"I don't follow you none," muttered the sheriff. "What you drivin' at?"

Tedro stabbed the moon-faced fellow with a look. "I've been tellin' you that Harmon Truesdale is the boss of the Black Ace herd. I've named others, and I've given you convincing proof to back up what I said. Sheriff, it's up to you to nail their hides to the fence!"

"Tedro Ames," said Potter steadily, looking the young cowpuncher straight in the eyes, "you're a danged outlaw. You kilt Thurston and Greenwald. You was forkin' Wolf Whalen's hoss. I sees only that you're tryin' tuh throw ugly s'picions on the finest man we got in our county, Truesdale. Yore hull story's a lie, and I wouldn't b'lieve a danged word you'd say on oath. Now go ahead an' shoot me, you killin' Black Ace!"

Tedro sat motionless looking at the officer a strangely baffled expression on his stubbled wind-chapped face. He said quietly: "If I was a killer I'd take an ax and split open your damned thick head and use it for kindlin'. Humn? . . . The way things stand you're just a nuisance to me and in my way, Potter. So—" He got up leisurely, stretched, drew his gun, walked over to the dugout door and unbarred it: "In here, Mister John Law!"

The sheriff looked at the gun, licked his dry lips and entered the dark underground hole. Tedro barred the door, stirred up the dying coals in the stove, put on fresh fuel and the kettle: "I'll have hot water for a shave after I come back from takin' Potter's hoss off this ranch. . . . Is the jasper really blind and dumb, or is he a Black Ace playin' his hand as he's been told to?"

CHAPTER NINE
TRIPLE DISASTER

At approximately four A.M. Henry Kline returned to his ranch, announced himself and called to Tedro Ames. The cowboy answered from the hay loft of the stable. This building backed up against dense willows along the little stream and had a rear exit. Thus Tedro could have reached the security of the willows at a moment's notice. He was taking no more chances of being trapped in the cabin. Now, stepping out to the yard, he inquired, "How'd you make out?"

Kline slapped his thigh triumphantly: "The Circle C wasn't bein' watched by any of the Black Ace pack. You see Mrs. Carter has paid the skunks every cent they asked for so as to relieve her mind and perhaps

139

save stubborn old Frank in spite of himself."

"Yes? How'd she get in touch with the killers?"

"Went out herself and nailed a half dozen notices to trees and posts round about the ranch sayin' she'd put the jack out in a certain place this evenin' and beggin' the devils to lay off. Mrs. Carter did all this herself, then made the rounds afore dark lookin' for some word from 'em.

"Writ on one of her notices was: 'O.K. Be sure you put the dough whar you sed and mind, no tricks.' So she allows they're safe now. Ol' Frank flat on his back don't know yet what she done. But when he finds out he'll jump off his bed spittin' brimstone. Say, man, them three cow waddies was some relieved, too."

"You fixed our business all right, Henry? Slim's on his way to—"

"You betcher life and daggoned glad to be swingin' into action, that cowboy. He sed he'd make Harpoon in four hours flat and burn up the wires once he got there. 'Course, Tedro, I never mentioned your name, jus' let on 'twas me and Sandy McKenzie as was so red-hot to get them telegrams sent and the Half Moon rannies back here pronto."

"This is Sunday mornin'," Tedro remarked thoughtfully. "Jess Walker and the Half Moon boys started on that wild goose chase, ridin' east from Harpoon, Friday. Two days on the trail. But they wouldn't hurry; had the grub wagon and the cavvy to hold 'em back, too. I calculate they won't be over a hundred miles, at the outside, from Harpoon. If only Slim can get hold of 'em by wire we can bank on their bein' at the Half Moon ranch before midnight tonight."

"Yes—if Slim gets hold of 'em this mornin' early," said Kline. "A big 'if' there—though I shore told Slim Shafter to be careful he didn't stop no hot lead—like poor old Ike Bowlaigs must have. . . . What the blazes'll them punchers do when they get here, Tedro?"

The old rancher was looking to young Tedro Ames for orders, advice, leadership. Leadership, a new rôle for Tedro, but he was accepting it and shouldering it well. He said: "I was doin' a heap of thinkin' and plannin' while I was usin' your dull razor. Why don't you ever get it honed?"

"Never mind. I use that razor to open cans with. My ol' face ain't so tender an' soft like yourn, an' you should ha' been catchin' you a nap 'stead o' shavin' anyhow. . . . You was thinkin'—?"

"Yes. Henry, the day after you were robbed when we smelled out the horse tracks—which same convinced us Truesdale was one of four thieves—you recall how one jasper rode west toward the mountains?"

Kline nodded. "Uh-huh. And that jigger was leadin' the nag he'd been usin' and ridin' the stockin'-legged bay hoss he'd just stole from you."

"He was masked when he helped hold us up," Tedro resumed, "but he did most of the talkin'. I was sure I'd heard his voice before. He looked sorta familiar, too. 'Fact, I was 'most certain then he was Wolf Whalen.

141

I'm dead sure of it, now."

"How can you be, son? . . . Still after you left me that Saturday afternoon you was aimin' to trail that feller, and then you was goin' to fog to Wind Ridge to leave a message for Ike Bowlaigs. Did—?"

"I trailed the bandit. The hoss he was leadin'—I knew its tracks—was Apache, the pinto I'd traded to Wolf himself. Well, I managed to follow the tracks into Flame Creek Canyon. Lost the trail plumb. Couldn't find it again. I made it for a mile or so up the canyon, then got stopped. Only somethin' with wings could go farther. Night was comin'. So I gave up and fanned the breeze to the lone pine on Wind Ridge—where plenty happened.

"Howsoever, the point I'm gettin' at right now is that *Wolf Whalen and Truesdale have joined forces.* Wolf and some or all of his renegades come from somewhere back in Flame Mountains at night to prowl the hills, obeying Truesdale's orders. Not hard to believe when we consider how many men have been dry-gulched. Now to get Wolf and his wolves, Truesdale and his hounds all in one bunch—and clean up on 'em!"

"Huh? You're daggoned ambitious. Have you figgered how it can be done? Tedro, I've shore underestimated you all these years. You're showin'—"

"Believe it can be done, Henry. First though, I collected another pet for our dugout collection of reptiles while you was gone—the brainy sheriff of Swiftwater."

142

"Uh? He one of 'em—the Aces?"

"Search me. But he's so darned stupid I don't think Truesdale would ever have taken a chance on lettin' him join the pack. Right now he complicates things."

"Yeh, but if he's square, get him on our side."

"Hell! I tried it. Nothin' doin'. Put your hoss up, Henry. I'll go over this idea I've got with you, then we'll get mighty busy afore daylight."

Henry Kline thought the idea was a "pippin, a lullycoola and a cracker jack." Ten minutes later he opened the door of the dugout and at the muzzle of his gun asked Boyd Loomis to come out. Loomis came defiantly, his eyes and expression both saying: "Go ahead, try and force any admissions out of me."

But it seemed the rancher and cowpuncher had no intention of questioning Loomis. Tedro promptly tied his hands, and then the two prodded the man to the stable, forced him to climb up to the hay mow, snubbed him to a post and left him.

Next, Tedro and Kline took Mooch from the dugout. Potter growled: "You fellows will sweat for this. Imprisoning an officer of the law's a penitentiary offence. Kline, you—"

"See you later," said the rancher and closed the door. "Well, Mooch," to the blanket-wrapped bar-fly who still had no clothing except his undershirt and drawers, "how 'bout comin' clean with us?"

Mooch shivered answering nothing at all. Kline shrugged, tied the fellow's hands, gagged him, put a gunny sack over his head and marched him up the trail two hundred yards from the buildings; there he tied him to an alder in the willows. Tedro meanwhile had made up two small packages of food; one for Kline, the other for himself. They rolled these in their slickers, took their rifles as well as their side arms and went out to the stable. As they saddled two horses they talked exultantly in low voices that yet would carry— to the hay loft.

"Mooch couldn't stand the gaff," thus Kline with a hearty chuckle.

"Coughed up a-plenty," said Tedro as if delighted. "Named every Black Ace he knows."

"Gave us a plenty to go on so we can locate Wolf's hideout, too," said Kline.

"Uh-huh, and afore sundown we'll have fifty men organized, not one of 'em a Black Ace either," said Tedro.

"And we'll comb this range pickin' up, or shootin' every daggoned one of 'em afore midnight t'night!"

"Hey, we shouldn't ha' said nothin'," Tedro suddenly warned in a tense voice little above a whisper. "I was that excited *I plum' forgot Loomis was in the loft!*"

"Me, too. I'll slit his throat right now!" Kline started up the ladder.

There was a rustle of hay, a scurrying of feet, then a plunk as a body hit ground at the rear end of the stable. Tedro leaped through the back door his gun out and flaming. But the dense willows had already hidden Boyd Loomis, who had found—possibly to his amazement—that he was not securely tied to the post after all. In the silence following the roar of Tedro's gun, Kline was shouting needlessly: "He's gone, the mow's empty!"

A few minutes elapsed before rancher and cowboy hit their saddles and left the stable. Two hundred yards upstream, they halted at the spot where Kline had left Mooch. The owner of the H K swung off and stepped back into the willows to get the bar-fly, whom he was going to take to the Circle C and have Frank Carter's wife and cowboys hide. As for the sheriff—somebody would find him in the dugout.

Of course the escape of Boyd Loomis had been planned in the hope that he—a Black Ace—would believe what he had overheard in the hay loft was indeed true. In this event, so Tedro and Kline had reasoned, the extortionists would band together for their mutual protection while they attempted to leave the country.

Tedro hoped, with the aid of the Half Moon cowpunchers, to block that move. However Jess Walker with his crew were far, far away and something might slip so they would not get home in time. Slim Shafter galloping down through the night to Harpoon to catch them by wire—oh, it was just a chance—and Tedro could not forget that Ike Bowlaigs had been stopped while on this same mission.

At this point the cowboy's reflections were interrupted. Henry Kline came bounding out of the willows. Day was just beginning to break and in the faint gray light Tedro saw the old timer's rugged face had turned as gray as the dawn.

"I tied him solid. So somebody let him loose," said Kline, as if he could not believe this was so. "It must ha' been Boyd Loomis as done it, and we'll never find neither one of 'em in this willow jungle. Mooch'll tell Loomis he never squealed, *that we don't know no more'n we did*. Tedro, your scheme's plumb blowed into a cocked hat."

"You mean," asked Tedro quietly though the muscles of his throat felt constricted, "Mooch has—?"

"He's flagged his kite!"

For a moment Tedro said nothing at all. Then: "Sometimes I wish I was hard-boiled. I should ha' tapped that coyote on the cabeza with an ax, such a lick as a fella'd give a beef intendin' to kill it first blow."

With a shrug he resumed, "So our little scheme goes haywire—if Truesdale believes Mooch when Mooch tells him he didn't squeal."

"Truesdale'll believe him all right," said Kline bitterly. "Also Boyd Loomis, if he's got hoss sense, will begin to figger how darned careless 'twas of us to let him overhear our talk; how mighty careless we was not to tie him solid, too. . . . Tedro, I needn't remind you we're fightin' for every square man in this neck of the woods. If we fail now the Black Aces will clean up and apparently vanish. But there'll still be Harmon Truesdale holdin' first mortgages on ranches and cattle, the notes comin' due and him demandin' they be paid."

"Truesdale won't live to collect," said Tedro quietly.

"Unless you shoot him, he will. Because you and me are the only men outside of the Black Aces who know what's what and who's who."

"We know what's what, but we lack a heap of knowin' all of the who's who," corrected Tedro. "Howsoever, I suggest that you go ahead with our plan, call on the old timers you know darned well you can trust and get 'em organized, then pick up or shoot Truesdale, Mooch, Boyd Loomis, the Stoddards and Greasy Holderness. You can trust the U. S. Marshal of course and I think you can gamble on Ray Thomas, and Postmaster Jim."

"I'll get busy pronto," returned the old rancher. "But what are you goin' to do?"

Tedro rolled a cigarette, lighted it, inhaled; his eyes on the Flame Peaks where the rosy light of sunrise on their bald crests warred with cloud mist. He was thinking, "Perhaps Truesdale, Loomis and others won't believe Mooch. They'll think he actually did come clean to me and Kline, for the fella's a jelly fish with no backbone. Perhaps, after all they will get scared enough to run. If so, they'll join Wolf Whalen and his outlaws, 'cause, sure as cows have horns, the bandits are workin' with Truesdale. They'll join Wolf and his crew for protection of numbers and to split the swag." Aloud he said:

"Kline, I'm goin' to see that old trapper, Silver-Tip Joe, on Swiftwater Pass."

"Eh?" sharply. "Why? A ride to Swiftwater Pass takes you twenty miles from the battle front—as it were. What good—?"

"Old Silver-Tip knows them mountains better'n any man livin'. Maybe he can tell me the most likely place to look for Wolf Whalen."

"And that," snorted the old rancher, "is the locoedest idee you've had till now."

"Wolf Whalen came from the west and the mountains, and headed back the same way after he stole the bay hoss he'd traded me," returned Tedro obstinately. "Silver-Tip's a crack trailer. Best in this neck of the woods. If he can't tell me where to locate Wolf, I'll bet he can smell out that jasper's trail. He's worth gettin' on the job. Be meetin' you t'night, Henry, at Pinnacle Rocks. Remember you're marked for death, same as I am now. Don't skylight yourself crossin' ridges and don't—"

"You needn't tell an ol' Injun fighter what not to do. So long, if you're dead set on this notion, and, yeh, 'tis worth while gettin' ol' Joe. Still you won't be back t'night, Tedro. Too much territory fer you to cover if you aim to prowl the top of Flame Range—a heap too much."

Watching Tedro Ames ride away the ranchman shook his head dubiously: "If I wasn't sartin shore o' the caliber o' that boy, I'd figger he was quittin'— aimin' to fan the breeze."

With this, Henry Kline, holding to deep valleys and to the cover of willows and timber, rode slowly to

Con Richards' ranch, the Slash R. This was the nearest place to his own and he had heard that Richards had received the dread spade-ace threat. Upon seeing only Richards himself, his wife and one hired hand at the buildings, Kline ventured to ride in boldly.

" 'Lo, Con. How's every little thing?"

" 'Lo, Kline." Richards surveyed his visitor stolidly. A plodding sort of fellow, past middle age, his family had grown up and deserted him. Deserted him, rumor said, because he was so downright stingy.

The hired man came across the yard from the corral with a pail of milk. Halting behind Kline's horse, he set the pail down and stood listening to his employer and the visitor. Mrs. Richards had appeared at the door of the house: "Glad to see you, Henry. Have breakfast with us."

"Will I be tickled to eat some o' your hot cakes, Mrs. Richards!" The old timer swung off, and then addressed Richards: "Con, me and Tedro Ames have got the low-down on some o' these Black Aces, so I'm—"

"Tedro Ames?" asked the ranchman quickly for him, and his heavy face began to redden with fury. "You hobnobbin' with that—?"

"Not exactly," Kline hastened to correct what he realized had been a mistake. Out of the corner of his eye he saw Mrs. Richards' figure stiffen, and he was suddenly furious. These fools condemned Tedro without knowing the truth.

149

"Here, here," he blurted. "Don't get all het up. Let me explain—"

"You can't explain nothin' 'bout that killer to me," rumbled Con Richards. "Arch Greenwald was my cowpuncher and a humdingin' good scout. Tedro shot him dead. Tedro's joined the bandits, was a-ridin'—"

Kline made matters infinitely worse: "'Twas Greenwald who went to the wild bunch. Tedro shot in self-defense and—"

"No! Arch had worked for us five years. Reliable, plumb! And what 'bout Tedro? He never held a steady job, he—say, I got it straight from Sheriff Potter and others—he's knowed to be one of them Black Aces."

"'Tain't so." Kline doubled his gnarled fist and shook it under Richards' nose. "Listen to me, Con. Us square ranchers got to get together; got to work fast and secret. I can name you six Black Aces. It's hard for you to believe, but Greenwald was one of the mob."

"I don't and won't believe it!" cried the woman from the doorway.

"Who else can you name?" asked Richards belligerently, and behind Henry Kline, unnoticed by him, the hired man stealthily drew his Colt .45.

"The Stoddards, Greasy—"

"Hell! Len Stoddard's got one of them spade-ace threats himself," roared Richards.

"—Boyd Loomis and Harmon Truesdale," Kline

plunged on. He saw Mrs. Richards give a violent start, drawing herself up as though stung by a wasp; heard her gasp, "That's a lie!"

"You've gone bughouse, Henry," Richards ejaculated. "Stand right still or George'll plug you!"

Baffled, the old settler stood still. Slowly he turned his head to see George with a big gun trained upon him.

Richards stepped cautiously to Kline's side and plucked the Colt from his holster. "We'll tie you and take you to town," he announced. "You're tryin' to pull wool over my eyes. You've throwed in with that devil, Tedro Ames."

Kline thought of several things to do, and did none of them, except explode into lurid profanity. A look into George's eyes told him the man would delight in shooting him—if he thought it necessary. In fact George demanded to know where he could find Tedro Ames. He wanted to even scores with Tedro for shooting Arch Greenwald.

The old timer pointedly ignored the question. "This plan's blowed into a cocked hat, like the other," he fumed as he was ordered to mount his horse. Then Con Richards and George tied him to his saddle and took him to Swiftwater, where it seemed only a moment before word ran like wildfire from mouth to mouth: "Henry Kline's been brought in tied to his hoss!"

From every business house and from the residence district people came swarming, men, women, children, to see what it was about. Strained and over-wrought already as were these citizens of Swiftwater, any new development in the Black Ace menace instantly caught their attention.

With a feeling of thwarted chagrin Kline observed Harmon Truesdale step out of the bank, followed by Boyd Loomis and Mooch. "So the pair o' little suckers has got to the big shark and reported a'ready," he gritted under his breath.

A bit farther along Editor Ray Thomas, eyes wild from the lack of sleep, hair flying as always and clothes mussier than ever, together with Jim Knowlton and a dozen others barred the street.

"Hold up, Richards," Thomas commanded. "Tell us what this means."

"Where's Sheriff Potter?" Richards countered.

"Not in town, but the U. S. Marshal's—"

"The U. S. Marshal? Good 'nuff. He's the man I'll turn this old fool named Kline over to."

Old Henry's smoldering eyes lighted with a ray of hope. If he could get the protection of this new man who'd come backed by the power of the United States Government, Truesdale and his mob would scarcely dare to shoot him or have him lynched. But Harmon Truesdale was striding purposefully to the group now surrounding Kline and his two guards. This crowd was growing every second, the Marshal not yet in evidence.

Ray Thomas looked at the old settler and in the newspaper man's eyes was a puzzled expression bordering on bewilderment. He said shortly: "Go get Marshal Ormsdale, Jim. He's at the hotel."

The crowd parted to right and left to let Truesdale through. In another moment the great man of Swiftwater, outwardly imperturbable, master of himself and easily the most commanding figure present, was looking calmly at Henry Kline. Truesdale's left eye was still black and swollen, though he had removed the bandage. He asked almost unconcernedly:

"What's the idea, Richards?" Then elevating his bushy eyebrows. "Is Kline a Black Ace?"

But the tone did not fool Kline in the least. This man was on tenterhooks, for Tedro Ames could be likened to a wolf gnawing at his vitals.

"You're dad-blamed right he is," rumbled Con Richards. "Leastwise he's hobnobbin' with Tedro Ames and protectin' him and believin' the locoed lies Tedro's a-tryin' to spread."

"They may not be lies, nor loco," spoke Ray Thomas.

Richards glared at the frowsy editor, resumed: "Why, Mr. Truesdale, this man, Kline, said—"

Postmaster Jim Knowlton came running back to the crowd; his lean face was as white as the new-fallen snow a-top Flame Peaks. He stopped, gasped: "Marshal Ormsdale's been knifed in his room at the hotel! He's dead!"

CHAPTER TEN

BETWEEN FLAME PEAKS

Night in Swiftwater Valley. The curtains of darkness hiding Flame Peaks, scarred buttes and hogbacks, wooded ridges, sagebrush flats and deep valleys. Clouds floating between earth and stars and a smell of storm in the still air. And through this soft velvety darkness Fay McKenzie trailed three outlaws by the sound of hoofbeats, often muffled, again sharp and clear.

The girl dared not get too close and yet wild horses could not have dragged her away from this exciting quest. She was doing something toward uncovering the hidden menace which had terrorized her country— the valley and the range where she had been born and which she loved—these many days.

Not so many days when she looked back on it. The extortionists had planned their campaign well and struck swiftly, decisively. Fair weather with clear days and moonless nights and the Half Moon outfit absent had aided them. Had Bill McKenzie been at home with efficient Jess Walker and the eight doughty cowboys the Black Aces would never have gotten as far as they had.

The Half Moon boys would have found signs and tracks which so far the sheriff and other men leading posses had failed to find. However what could one expect of such a duffer as Pete Potter? But—and the musing girl frowned thoughtfully—Len Stoddard was leading one party of man hunters. He was certainly efficient, a grim, hard man whom rumor said was absolutely fearless. Yet earlier today Stoddard had ignored Fay's pointed suggestion that he seek a hot trail on Wind Ridge. She wondered why and then stopped wondering about anything so distant and removed, for, momentarily lost in reflection, she had almost let herself be discovered by the outlaws she followed.

The sound of their horses' hoofs had ceased and she had been riding calmly on. Now she quickly halted, listened, hearing nothing except the far-away yelp of a lone coyote and the nearer at hand bellowed challenge of one bull to others of his kind. Range noises.

Ahead was a grove of dark cedars. She eased Torchy forward slowly, reached the trees, listened again and heard the faint squeak of saddle leather as horses in breathing moved the saddles. Fay slipped off, tied Torchy and stole through the trees. At the edge of the grove in the open stood four horses which indicated that the three bandits had been met by a fourth man. She saw the glowing tips of two cigarettes, smelled the smoke and then she heard indistinct voices.

Nearer crept the girl, heart thumping until she feared these riders of the night, of the owl-hoot trails, might hear it.

"What's new?" said one whom Fay realized was the

newcomer. "We-el, here's 'nother extra o' the Swift-water paper fer you to read when you get time. This Tedro Ames has got the big gun clawin' out his hair. I was t' tell you, Wolf, and you pass the word along, unless you can tie onto Tedro shore pop, he's tuh be shot dead at sight."

"Uh? Huh?" grunted Wolf Whalen rather blankly. "D'you mean he got away agin—got outa jail?"

"Jus' what I mean. Jake Stoddard was thar. He's nussin' a busted nose. Greasy Holderness is still feelin' sick tuh his stomach. That Tedro Ames is plumb hard tuh hold. Howsoever details o' his escape's in the paper, though the editor says nobody knows who put him in jail."

"Nobody but them as is s'posed tuh know," said Wolf dryly. "This wild man been seen since he high-tailed?"

"Yeh, I'll get tuh that in a minute, but here's an item in the paper I'll read you:

"'It seems that Mooch our well known bar room ornament, otherwise known as a bar-fly, decided to slip out of town last night. No one knows why. He must have been soused to the gills (You often are, Mooch) for he rode out in his underclothes. His outer rags were found tied to his saddle.

"'Mooch was headed off as he was crossing Swiftwater River by Sam Jones and Christy Mathers who were on sentry duty looking for

Tedro Ames. By a ruse he escaped from Sam and Christy (hard luck, boys. What if it had been Tedro!) and took their horses and fanned the breeze. He hasn't been seen since.'

"That's in Thomas' paper," said the squat, bow-legged man who was talking to Wolf and the other two outlaws. "What ain't in the paper is,—Say we gotta be ramblin'. We're due at the Slash R at nine tuh pick up four thousand bucks."

So interested had Fay McKenzie been that she almost called to the squat fellow: "What wasn't in the paper?"

The four bandits had mounted and were moving, Wolf asking: "Do we really pick up the swag or is there a killin' job fer you, Blazer?"

"No job fer me. The dope is, Con Richards is puttin' out the jack all jake. That's all fer us t'night, Wolf."

"Only four thousand," growled the boss outlaw. "Say, the big gun shore gets his hooks on most o' this dough. Scairt I'll double-cross him, maybe. . . . All fer us t'night, you sed?"

"Yeh. We're to go to yore camp soon as we can. I'll tell you why. Tedro Ames ain't been catched yet. He's got the goods on the big gun, got him scairt o' his shadder an' ready to fly the coop. So t'night—"

Fay was straining her ears and even moving after the four riders, but not another word could she catch.

"Who's the big gun that Tedro's got scared of his

157

shadow?" she whispered hurrying back through the cedars to Torchy. "Hooray! Somehow I never could entirely make myself believe Tedro had gone to the wild bunch!

"I wish I knew—dozens of things. I wish, how I wish I could see Tedro! But I'll help. I am helping. I'll—"

Suddenly she decided she would no longer trail the outlaws, for there was nothing she could do to prevent their robbing Con Richards of four thousand dollars. In fact she was glad he had complied with the Black Ace orders and saved his life. Blazer was one of the assassins of the terrorists. If Con Richards had not raised the money there would have been a job for him.

When they picked up the money the outlaws would be coming back this way! Therefore in the dense cedar grove Fay waited for their return. Perhaps yet tonight she'd find their hideout.

Some two hours elapsed before the same four men reappeared, riding unhurriedly past the cedar grove. But one, the youngest fellow, slender and not so very tall, halted and called: "Fellers, I got to fix my saddle blanket. She's slippin' agin."

"Yeh, them double Navajos is always rollin' out from under a feller's hull," Wolf said. "Catch up with us, Fuzzy, an' don't get lost."

Three outlaws rode on. Fuzzy dismounted and removed his saddle. He spread the blanket carefully and placed the saddle again on his horse's back. At this point Fay quite suddenly decided to do something really daring; something which might prove much safer for her than attempting to trail the outlaws.

To think was to act. She was among the dense cedars close to Torchy, hand on his nostrils. Abruptly she lifted her lariat from the saddle, flipped open a small noose, tiptoed closer to the bandit now cinching his saddle. As he straightened up a noose floated out of the timber, dropped neatly over his hat and was instantly jerked taut about his neck.

A fierce yank on the rope and Fay laid the astounded man flat on his back, strangled to such a degree that he could not voice a yell. The girl had roped and hog tied calves, colts and even larger stock. Deftly now she took advantage of Fuzzy's choked and momentarily dazed condition. Before he could get his gun—he was clawing at the noose with both hands— she jerked the weapon from his holster and tossed it aside.

Then with deft hitches she wound the lariat around and around the fellow pinning his arms to his sides. She stepped back, drew her own pistol and said: "Slide over to that nearest tree and sit with your back against it."

Gasping for breath, the man obeyed. Fay tied him to the tree, loosened the rope on his throat, wadded her own handkerchief in the outlaw's mouth and tied it in place with his bandana. She thought she should take the man's hat, but her own was almost as dark colored and as floppy. It would pass as well in the dark, so also would her jumper.

Leaving Torchy in the grove she swung up to the bandit's saddle on his late mount and spurred after the three outlaws going on up the ridge. One looked around as the girl took a place behind them, and asked: "Fix it?"

She felt she must answer something, so she hoarsely grunted, "Uh-huh," and wasn't she thankful that this reply seemed satisfactory. She held back a little to the rear. Fuzzy had been riding in that position when she had seen them, so now this also seemed satisfactory.

On and on moved the small cavalcade, a mile, perhaps two, the girl could not judge accurately, and then Wolf Whalen turned to the right and his mount with its rider vanished over the rim of the ridge. Behind the leader, the party formed into single file and Fay, the last one, found herself on an eyebrow trail running through dense timber and dipping sharply downward to a canyon. Very dark in these pines. She could scarcely see the rider ahead, but in occasional open areas the dark hats and silhouettes of the men were revealed. The murmur of a creek in the depths of this canyon became a gurgle and then a throaty chuckle. Soon the girl found herself riding up the bed of this water course itself.

She knew the stream, Flame Creek, fed by the melting snows on Flame Peaks. But she had never before known that one could ride up the canyon of this stream. The outlaw trail was not a trail known to the residents of Swiftwater Valley. How very dark it was in the deep canyon and the clouds, far above, had become heavier, darker, blotting out the friendly stars. A storm was brewing. Perhaps it would break before morning. Cold, too, Fay felt herself shivering. Often she lifted her feet clear of the stirrups raising them high when her mount plunged into pools breast-deep and deeper.

Often, too, the horse floundered and slipped on water-slickened boulders. A strange trail, hazardous, and suddenly the girl had panicky thoughts. Would she be able to find her way back? Yes, the horse would take her out of this wild country as it was now taking her into it. But if she did not get out, would Jess Walker be able to find and to follow this trail in the dark—or even by daylight?

She visualized Scottie the noble old collie galloping down through the night to the Half Moon; she saw him arriving, sore-footed, tired, panting, tongue lolling, and—and if the cowboys were not there what would Fay's mother, Tecumseh, the ranch hands think of the message? What would they do?

Of course it would frighten Mrs. McKenzie, but the girl now told herself she could not help it. The ruthless Black Aces must be trailed to earth and Fay had had the opportunity to trail them—at least a few of them. She would not be staunch old Bill McKenzie's daughter if she had lain down on the job.

The riders ahead of Fay had turned to the right once again and the girl's horse thankfully scrambled from the water to what Fay realized must be a huge flat rock. The horse shook itself like a dog, then across rocks—nothing but rocks—it hurried after the others. Fay looked back trying to mark this spot, but it was by far too dark for her to establish any definite landmark to guide her on the return trip. Now the horses were panting on a stiff upgrade, zigzagging back and forth on the wall of the canyon so steep that Fay thought of an expression of Tedro's: "R'ars right straight up and slants back a little."

Rocks loosened by clawing, clinging hoofs rolled down, down the sheer slope, ringing against other rocks, plunking against trees until finally the sound of their passing ceased in a muffled thump from far below. Up and up, climbing always, the riders reached the top of the canyon and came to palisaded rocks at the crest —apparently a solid wall six, ten, fifteen feet high. Surely, thought Fay, this is the end of the trail. We can't get over this wall. The outlaws were resting their heaving horses for a moment in the shadow of the palisades, high above the floor of the canyon.

A voice said: "Shore a bear-cat of a climb."

A match flamed, and Fay, ducking her head to shield her face, felt her heart stop.

"Put it out, Blazer, you damn fool!" snarled Wolf Whalen and the girl heard his hand strike that of the other man. Darkness again and again Fay dared to breathe. Blazer growled:

"My lungs is cravin' smoke, Chief, an' it's a cinch

they wouldn't be nobody see—"

"A man on t'other side o' this canyon'd see the flame of yore match," Wolf cut in harshly. "Le's go."

"Boss, you wasn't cautious none earlier t'day," commented the third outlaw.

"But Blazer told us plenty to make us wary as a pair of wolves with a litter of pups," the leader answered over his shoulder, riding onward. "Ye-ah, I'll say. The names of every Black Ace known to Henry Kline and Tedro Ames, and fifty cowboys, citizens o' Swift-water, ranchers bein' organized by that pair. . . . Damn a squealer!"

Fay's eyebrows went up. Could this be true? How she wished for further details. Blazer muttered:

"But they'll never find our trail or our lair, 'cause Mooch dunno the trail nor where at we're hid."

Conversation again ceased altogether. Westward along the base of the palisaded rock wall, Wolf led the way. The going was easier, the light better and Fay could see the three tough fellows more clearly. Abruptly the chief vanished. Then the next outlaw and the next. Fay reached the spot where they had disappeared and her mount took a right-angle turn through a notch in the wall.

For an instant it was scrambling, climbing like a cat, then it was out a-top the ridge, and the outlaws were riding on through timber once again. Seemingly only a stone's throw distant the two Flame Peaks lifted themselves against the dark sky. Storm clouds hovered over them. It was much colder. This was the high country. The trees, Fay knew, though she could not see them plainly enough to identify them, were no longer lodge-pole pines, but Engleman spruce. The biting air was pungent with their good, healthy smell.

Time passed, the horses sweating, panting as they climbed up the face of the mountain. Fay was tired and hungry, so hungry, and afraid, though she would not admit this to herself. She wanted to go back, but she must go on. Where, oh, where was the outlaws' hideout?

"Wisht we could get through the windfall," grumbled one bandit.

"Can't be did by nothin' but a bird," replied another. "Down logs back-high to a tall hoss and layin' every which-way."

Wolf Whalen turned to the left, through another gap in the rock parapet a-top the canyon. Down and down, weaving back and forth, sliding often, Fay's horse followed the others into Flame Canyon once more. What a trail! They reached the bottom, struck again the chuckling stream. But here the dark deep canyon was more open, wider, and here beside the stream ran a dim trail. A trail which came out at length, after the steepest climb of all, on the crest of the mighty range itself.

Fay found herself at the sources of Flame Creek, in the shadow of Flame Peaks, between these two hoary landmarks. Onward through a narrow gap between sheer rock walls rode the party and from nested boulders a-top the right hand wall a challenging voice came out of the dark:

"Password?"

"Lobos!" said Wolf Whalen.

"I knowed 'twas you, Chief, but had to challenge you anyhow," said the voice from the rocks.

"Correct, Stives," Wolf returned. "Don't ever forget to challenge and if they don't answer right, begin shootin'."

"I should turn back," ran Fay's tumultuous thought. "But if I do the sentry will see me. I'd be caught in no time."

Later she'd slip away afoot. Could she afoot find her way along the outlaw trail in the night? Very doubtful. It had seemed so simple, hours ago at twilight on the ridge when first she had seen the outlaws, to follow them, find their hideout and herself return. Now returning had been made anything but simple or easy.

She followed the bandits through the notch. It opened to a small oblong basin, surrounded by precipitous cliffs, shutting out all view of anything except the sky above and the snow-capped crests of both Flame Peaks. There were horses in the basin, a few scrubby trees, rank grass, some underbrush and running water. Over at the farther end close against the cliff was a fire, camp supplies, a tent and three tarp-covered beds. Beyond the camp lay an exit from the pocket to the west—just a narrow cleft or gap.

Four men, lounging near the cheery blaze had

turned their heads at the sound of horses approaching and Fay McKenzie seeing one of these felt her heart rise into her throat and stop beating. She was looking at the slab-shouldered, warped and weather-beaten old range veteran, Ike Bowlaigs.

Ike was cooking a meal at this late hour, nearly midnight, so evidently the bandits had forced him to work for them. That or— Fay dismissed the thought. Ike would never, never have turned outlaw. Suddenly, the full significance of Ike's being here struck the girl with crushing force and shock. Ike had never reached Harpoon. Her hope of getting Jess Walker and the cowboys on the job was gone!

A burly black-whiskered ruffian by the fire lifted himself to his feet, spat and called across the basin: "That you, Wolf?"

"Yep," said the boss, and reined up. "Unsaddle, men, and hobble yore hosses. Guess our new cookie's got chuck ready fer us." He chuckled grimly, "Wonder if the ol' coot's still snorty and rarin' to fight?"

Fay, a little behind the others, swung off. There seemed nothing else she could do. Her mind was a tumult. Ike here. She must get him away before this savage crew murdered him. Why had they not done so before this? Unexpectedly she got an answer. Blazer was speaking:

"Yore new cookie? Ike Bowlaigs, huh? I heard 'bout his bein' picked up as he fogged fer Harpoon. Why wasn't he shot?"

"You doan know the hull story then, Blazer?" the

brutal-faced outlaw who had been with Wolf when Fay had first seen the three outlaws, returned. "Wa-al, you see Len Stoddard met the ol' geezer, four—five miles south o' the Half Moon, and Ike, figgerin' he could trust Stoddard, 'course, up and told Len why he was fuzzin' tuh Harpoon—tuh send wires to Bill McKenzie and Jess Walker.

"Len knowed that wouldn't do, so he cracked down on Ike afore Ike knowed what 'twas all about. But Len Stoddard didn't want to kill Ike ner have him kilt, 'cause he didn't want his carcass found. You savvy, findin' the body'd tip off the gal of the Half Moon as her messenger got stopped. So Len had me bring him here."

"Yeh," said Blazer. "Why didn't you knock 'im in the head someplace 'long the trail?"

"Len sed tuh bring Ike yere," was the reply, "and I done it. Then Wolf sed, 'We'll make him dish up the chow fer us.'"

The men were taking the saddles from their tired, sweaty mounts—Wolf's the beautiful pinto, Apache, which Fay had once liked and desired to own. But a horse which she now hated because Apache had come between her and Tedro Ames. But she was not thinking of the pinto, nor of Tedro at this moment.

"Len Stoddard!" she whispered fiercely. "He drew his iron on Ike, had Ike brought here. . . . Len, of all men, and pretending to love me, asking me to marry him! Who can I trust? Who is or isn't one of the terrible mob? What a tangled maze."

167

She killed time by taking minutes to remove her saddle and rub her horse with the blanket. A girl alone in the outlaws' lair. A sentry guarding the east entrance. How to get out? How to save Ike? And perhaps more important for the moment how to keep from being detected herself?

Wolf, Blazer and the third bandit had walked to the fire. Their hobbled horses had rolled and started grazing. Fay looked at the group of men now in the bright firelight. Seven of them and Ike. What a tough, wicked-eyed, repulsive crew. Wolf was showing the others a small canvas sack and its contents. His voice came across to Fay beyond the circle of light.

"Four thousand bucks we picked up at Con Richards' place. Small change, boys. The big gun hisself, or Stoddard or Greasy Holderness, one, has managed to get 'round and grab off the bigger wads. . . . Hi, Fuzzy," calling to Fay, "never knowed you to fuss over a nag afore. Better come eat."

Fay answered no word. She adjusted hobbles she found on the saddle to her mount's fetlocks, still stalling for time.

"Chicken feed, ye-ah," one bandit answered Wolf. "We ain't a-gettin' the big dough—outside o' that twenty thousand you grabbed at the Half Moon, Wolf."

"Len and Jake Stoddard shore wanted me to turn that over to 'em," said Wolf in a brittle tone. "I tol' 'em where they could go. . . . But don't get anxious 'bout our split, men. The big gun aims to shoot square

168

with us. He may be here yet t'night."

"Huh? What'd bring 'im?"

"Seems like hell's popped out on Swiftwater Range. Blazer can tell you more'n I can. Tedro Ames has got the boss feelin' jus' as easy 's if he was settin' on a keg o' black powder with fire runnin' toward the powder. You tell the boys, Blazer. . . . Ike Bowlaigs, you got pie fer supper?"

"I got mulligan stew, you daggoned wall-eyed, snag-toothed rattlesnake," snorted old Ike. "An' I spiked it with stricknine what I had in my boot. You like stricknine, Wolf?"

"You talkin' sassy tuh me," roared the outlaw. "I'll—"

Ike lunged forward and hit Wolf a savage blow squarely on his hook nose. "Throw 'way yore shootin' iron," bellowed the old warrior, "an' I'll clean up on you with my fists and feet. I'll show you who's—"

A burly black-whiskered outlaw laid Ike flat by throwing an arm across his chest and tripping him backwards over an out-thrust leg. Wolf Whalen wiped blood from his nose, stepped back a pace, drew his Colt and rasped: "Get up so I can shoot you atween the eyes."

Out beyond the circle of firelight, Fay stifled a scream. Her pistol was in her hand, though she had no knowledge of having drawn it. She aimed at Wolf Whalen's head. She had never shot a man, but—

From down the little basin came a yell, the sentry's voice: "Wolf, men! Fuzzy's jus' come. There's a spy

169

yere! A spy rid in with you on Fuzzy's hoss!"

Wolf Whalen stood as though frozen. Frozen also were his men and Fay McKenzie. Ike had not yet scrambled to his feet. A horse thundered through the notch up into the gap. It dashed into the circle of firelight. It was Fay's pony, Torchy, and in the saddle the young bandit she had tied to a cedar. Words stampeded from the young bandit's lips:

"Get busy and hunt fer the jasper as rid here on my hoss!"

"Scatter and get 'im!" roared Wolf Whalen. "He's out thar in the basin yet."

Fay turned and ran blindly. A man would shoot it out with them, but she simply could not. She'd jump on a horse—any horse. She'd—. A pony leaped up beside her, her own Torchy. The rider, Fuzzy, left his saddle like a bulldogger. She felt his body strike hers. She was down and half smothered and the man had gripped her throat. Then Wolf Whalen and another bandit lifted the fellow aside. They caught hold of her, one by either arm, and dragged her to the fire. She saw Wolf's fierce eyes gazing intently into her face. Someone tore off her hat. She saw old Ike staring at her, his expression bewildered until he recognized her, then every vestige of color drained from his leathery face, while his eyes filled with stark fear.

"Why this jigger's a gal!" rumbled Wolf Whalen incredulously. "More'n *just a gal*. It's Fay McKenzie of the Half Moon!"

CHAPTER ELEVEN
YE EDITOR TAKES A HAND

Immediately following the postmaster's, Jim Knowlton's, announcement in Swiftwater, Henry Kline saw men's eyes and faces fill with fear and awe as they stared at one another, thunderstruck. He felt hope of protection or justice for himself ooze out at the toes of his worn boots. Ray Thomas broke the utter silence: " 'Twould seem Ormsdale must have got on the trail of something red-hot, and these curs of hell feared him, so they— Out of my way! I'm going to turn detective and look for clues." The editor fought his way clear and went flying up the street.

"The Black Aces stop at nothin'," a man yammered almost hysterically. "I ain't been threatened, but I'm going to pack and pull my freight outa this devils' country."

"I'll point out," said Truesdale significantly, "that we failed to catch Tedro Ames last night."

"That's so!" a voice cried. "You s'pose he stayed in town long enough for to get Ormsdale—with a knife?"

"Richards, don't look so bewildered," Truesdale snapped. "If you got reason to put Kline in jail, put him there. . . . Who's this and what—?"

Two horsemen had thundered into town. They dashed along Main Street toward the crowd and to his further dismay Henry Kline saw that one was Sheriff Pete Potter.

The horses thudded to a halt The sheriff shouted: "Who's that, tied to his hoss? Kline! By gosh that's good! Kline's a-workin' with Tedro Ames who's knowed to be a Black Ace thief and killer. Tedro locked me in Kline's dugout. Loomis and Mooch was there, too. But Kline and Tedro took them out to kill 'em, I s'pose. This mornin' along comes Denton, one o' my trusty men. He finds the H K deserted and he finds me in the danged dugout."

Con Richards called: "Glad to see you, Sheriff. . . . Take Henry Kline to jail. I want to get rid of him. I got plenty troubles o' my own, what with me gettin' a spade-ace card demandin' four thousand bucks. Four thousand, and I ain't got it. Got to borrow it."

"I'll lock 'im up, you bet," shouted Sheriff Potter. "Why there's Loomis and Mooch, too! How you jaspers get loose?"

"I got loose jus' in time to keep ol' Henry Kline from cuttin' my throat," rasped Boyd Loomis. "Him and Tedro Ames figgered to murder both me and Mooch. . . . Fellow citizens, this ol' hellion needs hangin', pronto."

Kline looked at Truesdale. Probably the boss had prompted his henchman, Loomis, to make this speech at the opportune moment. Naturally it would please the banker if Kline was summarily hanged. A voice was shouting:

"Yeh, if Kline's a Black Ace, swing him as an

example to the rest of the mob. But is he?"

Sheriff Potter whipped his horse through the bunched men, lined it up alongside Kline's. "Dry up that kind o' talk! There'll be no lynchin'. Out my way, fellers. I'm takin' Henry to jail."

"Good for you, Pete," offered the old settler. "You're the dumbest sonovagun on earth, but you shore got nerve."

Truesdale snapped his fingers saying crisply: "Yes, take Kline to jail, Sheriff. Hold him incommunicado until—until we sort of get organized. This savage butchery of the U. S. Marshal leaves us so shocked and numbed that even I cannot think clearly what to do next."

"What you mean, Mr. Truesdale, incom—com'-cado?" asked Potter blankly.

"Don't let him talk to anybody. You get me? Not to a living soul," grated the banker.

Potter nodded and the crowd opened allowing him to ride through with his prisoner. Kline observed the men frowning at one another in bewilderment. He knew that many of them, especially those who had known him for twenty years and longer could not believe that he had gone to the wild bunch. Yet in these hectic days they simply did not know what to believe.

Boyd Loomis and Mooch detached themselves from the bunched men and, following the sheriff, helped him to take Kline from his saddle. He realized that they hoped he would try to escape, so they could

173

have an excuse to shoot him. But the old timer was nobody's fool. He walked quietly into a cell.

Loomis lingered outside the door and when Potter's back was turned he whispered: "Mooch never squealed."

"Think not?" returned Kline, looking as wise as an old owl. He saw the other's expression change, and exultantly he realized that Boyd Loomis did not know for sure but what Mooch had talked.

"Where can we find Tedro Ames?" Loomis demanded.

"Hi, come way from thar, Loomis," commanded the sheriff. "You heard my orders. This prisner's tuh be held incom—uh— You ain't to gab with him. Get out, you jaspers."

As Mooch and Loomis went out Potter stepped to the cell door, favored Kline with a triumphant malignant glare and truculently demanded: "Where'll *I* find Tedro?"

"I want breakfast immejitly, Sheriff. I like my java strong and black 'ithout no fixin's. I want a quart of it, sody biscuits and beef steak with gravy."

The sheriff swore then growled, "I'm goin' to take on a feed myself, but I'll feed you when I get 'round to it." He stamped out slamming the office door behind him.

The town was buzzing, both men and women more excited and more wrought up than at any time yet since the start of the extortionist menace. Some fami-

174

lies were getting ready to leave for Harpoon or other points until the danger was past; others were airing their views and theories, but no one was doing much of anything about it except talk and look at Truesdale and Potter for leadership.

That is no one was doing anything definite about the situation except Ray Thomas, editor of the *Swiftwater Star*. Thomas was in the upstairs room at the Swiftwater Hotel where Marshal Ormsdale had met his death. With the editor was Harry Ayres, proprietor of the hostelry, the coroner and Postmaster Jim Knowlton.

Thomas had turned everything in the room bottom-side up, even to looking under the rug and moving the bed with the grisly body upon it. He had searched Ormsdale's night garments and his clothing thoroughly. The murderer might easily have entered by either the window or the door, but he had left no tracks. Now Thomas rested, tossed his head and ran his ink-stained fingers through his hair, causing it to stand out from his head in wilder confusion than ever.

"Gentlemen, I'm a flop as a Sherlock. I can't look wise and say, 'Ah! Most interesting.'" Changing manner and tone he went on: "The dirty skunk of a knifer took his weapon with him; took also the envelopes and other papers with samples of handwriting on them and the spade aces that Jim Knowlton furnished. I ain't—haven't—found a darned thing that looks like a clue. How about you, men?"

The coroner shook his head. Ayres, who'd been wringing his hands and glooming about such a terrible thing taking place in his hotel, muttered: "You believe that Ormsdale discovered something so important that these unknown and unnamed devils had to silence him?"

"That's the inference," Thomas returned. "Say, you was up most all night wasn't you, Ayres? Didn't you hear anything—the assassin come in the back way in the wee small hours fer instance?"

"No. But I dozed off there in the office after midnight. Hit the hay little after three."

"I was getting out an extra, working full blast at my shop," said Thomas. "But after the excitement over Tedro's gettin' away died down Ormsdale dropped into my den for a spell. He had the cards and stuff Jim had given him; said he was working on the handwriting, trying to find out who wrote or writes the Black Ace threats. I couldn't talk with him, and he left about eleven or twelve. You see him come in, Ayres?"

The proprietor nodded. " 'Twas at twelve. Ormsdale woke me to get his key. He went to his room."

"And that was the last time you saw him alive?"

"No. About three this mornin'—the clock had just struck—Ormsdale came down stairs quiet like—"

"Yes, yes!" Thomas was all eagerness.

"There was starlight in the lobby comin' through the windows and he came over to me, gripped my shoulder, said, 'Here's a big envelope I'd like to put in your safe.' So I opened up the little safe and he put his envelope in it. He went back to his room and I heard his door shut. . . . Where you goin', Thomas?"

"Downstairs. Come on!"

As the four men rushed down the stairs, Thomas ahead, Ayres resumed: "Well, I went to bed few minutes after that."

"Open up this strong box," commanded the editor, leading the way to the safe in a corner behind the counter.

Harry Ayres twirled the knobs. The safe door swung wide, all four men holding their breath. "Where's Ormsdale's envelope?" demanded Thomas.

The hotel man looked up blankly. "It ain't here! I've been robbed of all my cash too!"

"Damn!" snapped Thomas. "Who are these devil's stepchildren? Are they watching everything, watching us now?"

The coroner, Ayres, and the postmaster glanced quickly, apprehensively about them. Said Jim lowering his voice: "Thomas, ye suppose Ormsdale found out who's the penman that writes the Black Ace threats?"

"Yes. Why, why didn't he come to me and tell me? What a story for the paper. What a scoop. 'Identity of man who writes Black Ace threats known!' "

Through the window, across the street, the editor saw a man stop and gaze fixedly at the hotel. It was Harmon Truesdale. Immediately he crossed the street and Jim Knowlton opened the door to admit him.

"What a headline!" Thomas ejaculated. "Identity of man who writes Black Ace threats known!"

"Is that true, Ray Thomas?" asked the banker.

"No, Mr. Truesdale. I was just thinking of what might have been if Ormsdale had come to me, or if he hadn't been—"

"Murdered by one of those fiends," interrupted Truesdale, his voice bitter. "Men, this situation is simply hellish." He left the hotel and with dignified step strode down the street.

Ray Thomas stepped to the sidewalk, watching the banker until he was out of earshot, then he turned to Jim Knowlton saying:

"It's queer. The queerest sensation I ever felt. When Truesdale asked me that question I had a feeling he'd kill me on the spot if I answered 'yes'. It was in his eyes."

"You're goofier'n ever," muttered Ayres, the hotel man.

But Jim Knowlton said huskily: "I swan, Ray, I had that same feeling!"

In jail Henry Kline spent the bitterest day of his sixty-odd years. He had been in tight spots before but never one so tight and unpleasant as this. Of course Truesdale and some of his men would take him out and shoot him as a rancher would shoot a wolf sooner or later. The puzzling thing was why they were delaying the job—probably waiting for the cover of darkness.

Kline fumed helplessly. Here he was wasting all valuable time when he should be organizing honest ranchers to wipe out the extortionists. Organizing ranchers? Hell! The first one he had approached had disbelieved him and taken him prisoner. Henry Kline would hesitate before he told his story to any other ranchman. The only hope now of immediately cleaning up on Truesdale and his crew lay in the Half Moon cowpunchers. But Kline reflected with profane disgruntlement, if Jess Walker and his rannies reached the Half Moon this evening, they would not know what to do. Slim Shafter could tell them many things, but not the all-important things. Slim knew not the identity of any of the Black Aces.

Kline swore again. He must get out. Otherwise— But escape seemed utterly out of the question. All day long Sheriff Potter, the misguided bonehead, rode close herd on the jail and his prisoner. True to his instructions from Truesdale, Potter allowed no one to speak with Kline. Visitors were decidedly not welcome and Potter enforced his "keep out" orders with his gun. "Skeedaddle or I'll shoot the legs off you."

Night at last and staunch old Henry Kline felt the clammy sweat of despair. There'd be something doing soon and his chances of seeing another sunrise were equal to those of a crippled steer surrounded by six hungry wolves. However he was not long kept in suspense.

Potter had lighted his lamp and sat with his boots

on his desk smoking a cigar with a self-satisfied smile on his flat moon face as if to say, "I'm doin' my duty like Truesdale said." Most abruptly the office door opened and framed for a moment a darkly clad masked man with a huge cap pulled low on his head. In this phantom's hand was a very large gun and it pointed straight at Potter's left ear. The door swung shut.

The sheriff's feet hit the floor with a thump. Otherwise he sat very still with his hands shoulder-high. The masked man uttered certain decisive, terse orders in a disguised voice. Potter lifted his bulk slowly, carefully, walked to the wall and stood against it hands now reaching to the ceiling. The intruder removed the sheriff's. belt, handcuffed his hands behind his back, gagged him and then he opened Kline's cell door with Potter's keys.

"In with you, Sheriff. Out with you, Kline."

Potter entered the cell. The rancher came out.

The masked man closed and locked the cell door. He handed Henry Kline the sheriff's belt and gun. "Horses out back. Hurry!" he whispered.

Mystified, the rancher buckled on the belt, felt the comforting weight of a filled holster against his thigh. This was mighty queer. The Truesdale crew would surely never give him a gun. But the masked man had blown out the lamp and was going through the door. Kline followed.

The two, rescued and rescuer, stood close together for an instant, both watching the same thing in the dim light. Some fifty yards distant five horsemen had reined up.

"So that's the play!" thought Kline. "I'm let outa the jug so they can mow me down, sayin' later I was caught attempting a jail break." His left hand viced the masked man's shoulder; his right jerked loose the Colt so recently acquired. He gritted:

"Leadin' me to a trap, huh? I'll jus' use you for a shield."

Low words struck his ears. "Henry, this is Ray Thomas and I'm on the level with you."

Kline knew the voice at last. It was Thomas! His hand fell: "Lead us to the hosses!"

The editor scooted around the jail, Kline at his heels. Fifty yards distant a voice yammered, "Jail went dark suddent. I see somebody. *He's gettin' away!*"

"Cut loose!" snapped a terse order.

Five horses tornadoed forward. Fire flashed from flaming guns. Bullets splattered against the solid wall of the jail, screamed as they ricochetted. Kline and Thomas were behind the building now, running on to another. The horsemen split to right and left charging around the jail.

"There they go!"

"Drop 'em. Riddle 'em! No matter who the second man is!"

Hot lead whistled all around the two men, thudded into the earth. They reached the farther building, darted around a corner and found two frightened horses. Kline jerked loose the bridle reins of one and was up in the saddle. As his mount leaped forward he looked back. Thomas, no cowboy and unused to this sort of thing, was having trouble. Kline whirled his mount back, caught hold of his ally and literally picked him up tossing him astride the horse. A rider loomed up alongside them, but his gun hammer echoed dully on an empty shell and he cursed, swinging the gun at Thomas' head. The blow missed. Another rider was coming, his Colt spitting flame and leaden death.

The shot went wild and the fugitives were off at breakneck speed northward out of Swiftwater. Five men thundered in pursuit. Kline pulled his weapon, fired under his left arm five times in rapid succession. One pursuer swayed in his saddle, his mount veered aside. Another horse crashed down and a third smashed into it turning a somersault. Instantly the two remaining riders pulled up. On dashed Kline and editor Thomas.

Half a mile wordlessly riding as fast as their horses could run, then suddenly Kline swerved to the right, led the way into a dense aspen grove. Both horses stopped. The two men watched four riders zip on northward.

"I sure owe you plenty fer this, Thomas," said Kline huskily.

"Nothing at all, Henry. Glory! I never had such a thrill. I'd do it all over again."

"You would, huh? How'd you get wise?"

"Tedro Ames. You really owe your life to him."

"The hell you say. How'd Tedro—?"

"Of course, understand, I'd have bet my last blue chip that neither you nor young Ames had gone to the wild bunch, and early today something came up in connection with my investigation of the marshal's death to cause me to do a lot of thinking about Harmon Truesdale. 'Twas—"

"But about Tedro?"

"Oh, yes. At twilight this evening that old trapper, Silver-Tip Joe, arrived in town in his buckboard. He'd cut his left foot with an ax recently and was needing medical attention."

"Yes, yes. Hurry up, feller. You ain't writin' the full details now."

"But before Joe went to see the doctor, he limped to my shop to give me a letter from Tedro."

"Joe's crippled, uh? Bad when Tedro was countin' on him. What was in the letter?"

"Tedro wrote me what he knew about the Black Ace mob, how Truesdale, the leader, was working with the outlaws. He said, 'There'll be plenty of men trying to kill Kline. I can only hope they fail. But if they do drop Henry and me I want somebody to know the truth as far as we two—and now Silver-Tip Joe— know it. Get such men as you know you can trust organized and get in touch with Henry, pronto. And for God's sake don't fail us, Thomas.'"

Kline whistled softly. "So that was the way of it. And you believed Tedro?"

"What a question when I just took you out of jail! I didn't have time to get anybody else to help and Joe, being so badly crippled couldn't—to his chagrin."

"Silver-Tip Joe say where Tedro is tonight?"

"No, he didn't say. . . . You know, Henry, it was the Stoddards, Boyd Loomis, Mooch and Greasy Holderness who just tried to kill us both. Proof enough to me that what Tedro said was right."

"Put 'er there, friend," said Kline, extending his gnarled hand. "You'll do to take along, even though you're an ink-slinger, not a gunfighter. Now we'll circle back and ramble to the Half Moon ranch."

"Yes, to the Half Moon. Tedro didn't put it in his letter, but he had Joe tell me we could bank on Bill McKenzie's cowpunchers. You lead, old scout. I'll try to follow."

CHAPTER TWELVE

A COLLIE AND THE COWBOYS

There was excitement at the Half Moon ranch on Swiftwater River at the mouth of Trails Rest Creek that Sunday night long before old settler Henry Kline and Editor Ray Thomas got there.

In the first place, the two ranch hands and the blacksmith had gone to town before noon and in Swiftwater they had learned astounding things of which, curiously, or perhaps not so curiously when Fay McKenzie and Ike Bowlaigs both had done all in their

184

power to keep news of the Black Aces from Mrs. McKenzie and consequently from the men, particularly W. T. S. Johnsing Brown—they had heard only vague rumors.

Learning how they had been left out of things the blacksmith and one ranch hand had promptly elected to stay in Swiftwater waiting for new developments in this strange weird war. But the chore man had been obliged, most reluctantly, to return to the ranch to do the milking, feeding of calves and pigs and other absolutely necessary chores. He arrived shortly after dark fairly bursting with news and for the first time Mrs. McKenzie with Tecumseh learned of how the erstwhile peaceful, prosperous range country had been taken over by phantom riders of the night.

Unknown terrorists who sent honest men threats always on spade aces, and who mercilessly shot from the dark those who failed to comply with the demands written on these sinister cards. The darky cook clutched his rabbit's foot with both hands. His white eyes rolled; he could prepare no supper that night and had it not been dark he would have fled, not to Swiftwater, but to Harpoon.

Mrs. McKenzie in rather delicate health, but at the same time a pioneer woman who had come to the valley twenty-two long years ago when it was still mostly unsettled, wild and untamed was inclined to scoff, frankly discrediting the chore man's wild stories. She had seen her share of range wars, had experienced even a brush or two with hostile Indians yet never had she heard or dreamed of anything like this. That such a thing could happen in a settled community where they had law and order and a sheriff seemed utterly incredible.

However, she at once asked what had become of Ike Bowlaigs whom she had thought was back in the hills gathering straggling bunches of cattle missed by the roundup. The chore man had no least idea of what had become of Ike. And then Mrs. McKenzie became alarmed indeed, thinking of Fay. Before nine this morning the girl had left—to ride in the hills. She had not yet returned. It would not be like Sandy to stay all night at some other ranch and leave her mother alone. Besides in the rough hills and mountains to westward and northward there were no ranches.

Mrs. McKenzie reassured herself that Sandy had taken Scottie along. The faithful old collie would lead her back home if she had gotten lost. But as the minutes dragged past, seemingly leaden and still the girl did not appear even this pioneer woman grew almost as chilled with fear as Tecumseh Johnsing Brown.

Suddenly the two remaining dogs began to bark, and dramatically out of the dark into the lane of light streaming from the ranch house door came a bedraggled, sore-footed and panting collie. It was Scottie. His mates greeted him vociferously, nudged him with their wet noses, but he limped to his mistress and threw himself down at her feet, tongue lolling, his body one great quiver of exhaustion, but his bright eyes gazing up to Mrs. McKenzie's face as if he was trying to tell her something.

As the trembling woman bent to pat his head, the chore man came running from the corral, and Tecumseh reappeared after having locked himself in his own quarters the moment the dogs began to bark.

"Scottie home without Miz Sandy," whispered the chore man in a scared voice.

"Yes. What's this?" Mrs. McKenzie had found Fay's glove tied to Scottie's collar. She released it, shook from the glove a small note book. "Is it a message from my little girl? I wonder—"

She steadied her nerves, opened the tiny book and read:

"Mumsy, I'm all right and don't you worry. This is to Jess Walker, Ike and the other cowboys. I've found the outlaw trail—tracks of horses where they come from the mountains—and I know it's Wolf Whalen's trail because I saw him and two more bandits. I'm going to follow them and learn the trail."

Mrs. McKenzie dropped the message: "She's going to follow the bandits!"

The chore man wet his lips, picked up the little book and tendered it to her. Tecumseh gulped, "Lawsy!"

"I'm now on the ridge directly south of Flame Creek and approximately five miles west of

Swiftwater Valley. Jess, come to this ridge and follow up it. I'll try to meet you right along here. Come, because these outlaws are a part of the Black Ace crowd. I know this. We must get them."

"That's all," said the woman hollowly. "Oh, to think of Sandy trailing those— What will we do?"

The chore man's Adam's apple ran up and down his long throat. He said, "I shore dunno."

"But where are the cowboys, and Ike?" cried Mrs. McKenzie. "They should have been home—why, they should have come Friday night."

As though in answer to her question out of the south along the highway sounded the steady rhythmic thump and pound of hoofs; a sound of horses ridden hard and far loping steadily, doggedly. Mrs. McKenzie was soon at the outer gate with a lantern. She swung the gate wide. It was the Half Moon cowboys. Lean and leathery old Jess Walker with his flowing copper-colored mustache ahead; riding beside him the slender, wiry and blond Slim Shafter.

Slim Shafter who was not a Half Moon cowboy, but was none the less a man whose name when the story of those dread days in Swiftwater Valley was all told went down in history as a hero. This heretofore prankful, happy, twinkling-eyed ranny had ridden the morning star out of the sky galloping south and ever south to Harpoon on a mission. In the gray light of dawn Slim Shafter had trailed his noisy spurs across the threshold of the telegraph office at Harpoon and behind the rider an iron-hearted horse of the Circle C brand had hung its head to the ground, gasping, choking for breath; a wringing-wet and lathered horse dying on its feet.

This at daybreak and Slim Shafter's telegram had caught the Half Moon cowboys approximately one hundred miles east of Harpoon. But Jess Walker, wise and experienced old head, had not seen fit to kill horses in any world's record ride back to the Half Moon. Instead Jess had at once seen about a west-bound freight train.

He had loaded a stock car with ponies, left the cook and the wrangler to bring the wagon and the rest of the cavvy, while he and the other punchers rode the caboose behind this freight train. Harpoon at five-thirty and there at the stockyards was Slim Shafter to tell the cowboys what the call was all about and why "Sandy" had sent for them to "come-a-hellin'!"

And here they were, Jess and Slim with seven efficient rannies just four hours out of Harpoon forty long miles away. Each man had a rifle, boxes of ammunition and full belts of six-shooter shells. Slim Shafter had bought the rifles and the ammunition in Harpoon. Slim had also caught old Bill McKenzie by wire and had gotten an answer. McKenzie had purchased no cattle at Prairie Owl, and he'd be right on guard against "two yahoos" who'd ridden the stock train with him eastward to market from Harpoon. His reply ended: "Rest easy, Sandy." For Tedro had signed his messages, "Sandy" and Slim had most certainly not seen fit to change this.

Now, riding through the gate at the Half Moon, Jess Walker said: "Hello, Mrs. McKenzie. . . . Where's Sandy?"

The answer came with a sob half of relief, half of fear. "Jess, she's after trailing outlaws."

Then Mrs. McKenzie told of the message brought by Scottie and what it had said.

Staunch old Jess Walker and the cowboys listened.

"And oh, Jess, do you think those bandits will catch my little gir-r-l?"

"Not a chance," returned the foreman gruffly to hide his real thoughts. "Sandy's able to take care of herself any place. . . . Change hosses, boys, pronto."

"To these we're leadin'?" asked one rider.

"No. To fresh broncs. Two of you wrangle and whoop it up." Foreman Jess stepped from his saddle and walked stiffly over to where Scottie lay still panting in the light from the house. He squatted beside the faithful dog and rubbed his head and ears and Slim Shafter, coming also to pay his respects to the collie, heard the hard-bitten, leathery old foreman say very huskily: "Scottie, ol' feller, you'll do to ride the river with!"

Thudding hoofs in the dark, a cavvy racing into a corral, a gate slamming behind. Cowboys with ropes, picking out the fleetest and the toughest mounts. Tecumseh Johnsing Brown, suddenly calmed and become again efficient, shouting: "I's throwed canned grub together an' got hawt cawffee, boys. Feed yor' faces 'fore you go."

"Good idea, but don't take more'n three minutes," boomed the foreman, and the riders took scarcely more time to swallow scalding coffee and gobble beans, tomatoes and cold bread. Some ate with one hand while slapping sweat-soaked saddle blankets upon horses' backs, and sweat-soaked saddles on top of the blankets. They cinched up, mounted, nine efficient fighting men. Came a brief interlude while five fresh and "salty" horses tried to buck off their riders and while Jess Walker spoke reassuringly to troubled, but brave Mrs. McKenzie.

Then came yet another momentary pause. Drumming hoofs from the north. Two riders pulling up at the gate and a voice calling: "Who all's there?"

"Jess Walker, Slim Shafter and the Half Moon crew. Who're you?" challengingly.

"Thomas, by grab, it's O.K. They're here!" roared Henry Kline. He rode through the gate, trailed by editor Ray Thomas. "Hi, Slim Shafter. You did it!"

"Uh-huh. What's new, Henry?"

"Plenty. Where you fellers headin'?"

Jess Walker told him and told him why. Kline nodded grimly. "Lead out. That's where we'll go—to meet Sandy. I had a notion o' roundin' up a passel of skunks in Swiftwater, but that's off for the present."

Forward under the dim stars in a cloudy sky across the rough hills following no trail at all. Kline rode ahead with Jess and Slim and he talked, anticipating questions. Ray Thomas, still thrilled as never before in what he called his eventless life, rode behind with the other punchers and he talked. . . . "And so you see, cowboys, Tedro Ames is the man who has thrown the monkey wrench into Truesdale's smoothly working, diabolical scheme. No wonder Truesdale now offers five thousand bucks for Tedro's scalp.

"Boys, that fellow must realize he's sitting on a keg of dynamite. My fear is that while we are chasing after the outlaw part of this hellish crew Truesdale and the other villains we know of will escape."

"Maybe, but we'll run 'em down—after we find Sandy," Jess called back.

"Golly! How I wish we had Tedro with us," said Kline. "Jess, that cowboy has become a regular bear-cat on wheels. Took somethin' terrific, like this deal, to jolt him into showin' his mettle. But t'night I dunno where he is even. He'd be powerful glad to know Sandy found the trail he hoped to find."

"Yep," agreed the foreman. "Be darned hard on Tedro not to be in at the show-down. Too bad."

At midnight the grim riders reached the ridge Sandy had designated and the girl was not there. They trailed up along it single file, but, due to the darkness and because they did not know the outlaw trail, they passed the place where Wolf Whalen had turned down the slope to the right when Fay had ridden with the bandits. Soon discovering their error the cowboys returned to the last spot they had seen horse tracks and this time found where the trail—if such it could be

192

called—led downward into the depth of lower Flame Canyon.

Kline, the most experienced woodsman and tracker rode ahead and he "smelled out the trail" to the bottom of the chasm and up it in the stream. Then he missed the spot where the outlaws again turned to the right leaving the water. In the Stygian darkness of this canyon the riders found themselves stuck. Travel any farther up the canyon had become impossible even to a man on foot.

"They must ha' swung out either to the right or left," said the old timer. "We got to find where."

They prowled in the dark to the right and left of the creek floundering, on foot, over underbrush, fallen logs, rocks, and at last drew together, baffled.

"Seems like we jus' gotta wait for daylight," growled Jess. "Wonder where at's Sandy? . . . Lord, if anything'd happen to her!"

"Quiet, everybody. Hold your hosses' nostrils, too," came Slim Shafter's tense whisper.

In another sixty seconds the men heard what he had heard before they did—the rustle of branches on trees, the sharp clack of shod hoofs striking rocks!

Down country, below them, was another party of horsemen, and these fellows knew where they were going. Quickly Kline and Jess left the other punchers and stole forward afoot, and though they could not see the newcomers they heard them climbing the north wall of the canyon. Jess went back to his men to lead them. Kline hurried after the unseen riders keeping track of them by sound. Riders who unwittingly and unknowingly were setting the old timer, Ray Thomas and the Half Moon cowpunchers on the right trail!

CHAPTER THIRTEEN
THE MAN OUTSIDE

Silver-Tip Joe lived a-top the mountain world. Twenty miles of trackless country—darkly forested slopes; crags, pinnacles and ridges that upreared themselves above timber line; hoary peaks tipped with snow the year long; moraines and lakes; chasms dark and mysterious—lay between the trapper's habitation and Flame Peaks, higher than all other landmarks along Flame Range.

Much nearer to Joe's cabin, within a half mile in fact, lay the road which followed up Swiftwater River from the valley, out east, to reach the crest of the range by way of Swiftwater Pass. This road, scarcely more than a pack-horse trail, though teams could negotiate it, twisted and wound onward across the mountains skirting impassable places, finally to enter another canyon leading down the western slope of Flame Range.

It was but little traveled at any time, which as a usual thing bothered Trapper Joe, who loved solitude, not at all. But on this particular morning he was anxiously scanning as much as he could see of the trail hoping someone, almost anyone, would "drift along". Aha, a rider had appeared coming from the east. Silver-Tip dropped his home-made crutch, leaned against his door frame and cupped his hands to his bearded lips to whistle.

But there was no need. The black-hatted rider had turned his horse towards Joe's stout log cabin, built to withstand winds and storms of the high country.

" 'Lo, there, Silver-Tip," greeted Tedro Ames, while yet a hundred yards distant. Then with sudden dismay: "What the blazes ails your left foot? Daggone it, you can't be crippled right at this time when I'm—we're needin' you bad."

"But I'm lamer'n a fox in a Number Four trap, and almoughty glad you drifted in yere. How air you, kid? . . . Hey, where's your striped pants, your calf-skin vest an' your big white hat? . . . Heh-ho, you looks somethin' like a real honest-tuh-gawsh cowpuncher now. Why the change? What's—?"

"Never mind the hoorawin'," Tedro reined in, swung off and mustered a grin, though he had never felt less like smiling. "What's matter with that foot?"

"Aw!" Silver-Tip swore testily. "I was a splittin' firewood, and—"

"Standin' on a hunk of it and whackin' away with your ax like a greenhorn," flashed Tedro.

Silver-Tip's nose reddened. This was practically all that could be seen of his face except his keen steel-grey eyes undimmed by advancing years. Some said this old bear hunter—he had brought in the hides of more silver tips and smaller bears than any man in the region—was over eighty, but no one, not even Joe himself knew for sure. Just as no one knew what he would look like if he ever visited a barber. He never had. Beard and hair, both greying now, grew wild and long, unkempt and uncombed.

"Uh-huh," he muttered. " 'Twere a tenderfoot stunt, sure 'nuff. My ax slipped, cut right through my boot and sock inter the bone thar on my instep. Dad-blame it all, that were three days ago. I thunk she'd be all jake, slapped a hunk o' moist terbaccer on the ol' hoof an' wropped 'er up. But—"

"Inside," ordered Tedro, placing one arm about the old man's shoulders and half lifting him into the cabin. "Sit on your bunk and let me look at this foot."

"Huh? You can't do 'er no good. I was 'bout to tell you, 'tain't comin' jake. Sorer'n a bile; cayn't set 'er to the ground. Laig's swole, too."

"I can see that. Look here, ol' whiskers, you've got to go to a doctor, or—"

"I had the same idear, Tedro. You see there's proud flesh startin' to grow in that gash. Daggone. I'd a-hooked up an' driv to town only you know that pesky hawse o' mine an' that dad-blamed foxy mule—they're grazin' in yander little meader—but you think I could catch 'em with me crutchin' 'round? Naw sir, kid, them nags give me the hawse laugh and the mule hee-haw. . . . Hey, doan you throw that rag 'way. It's the onliest one they is."

"Snorty Cow! Is it? Just the filth on that rag was

plenty to infect the cut without your old reliable tobacco remedy. . . . Any turpentine?"

"Nope."

"Anything else that'll do for a disinfectant?"

"Huh? What you mean?"

Tedro looked around helplessly. "I've got nothin' to clean the wound with. Neither have you. It's infected. Liable to cause blood poison; you savvy that?"

"You bet your boots I savvy blood poison and proud flesh, but not 'bout disin—what? But, I ain't feelin' dizzy ner nothin'. I can drive all jake. You catch that smart-alec team an'—"

"Just what I was going to do." Tedro caught the mule and the horse, hitched them to the ancient buckboard and then mentioned why he had come to see the trapper.

"What's all this?" demanded Silver-Tip. "Fust I'd hearn tell of—what you call 'em? Black Aces? Tell me the hull thing."

Tedro was glad to unburden himself to this old-timer whom he felt sure he could trust. Furthermore Silver-Tip might prove an invaluable ally even though crippled: "Now you see why I wanted you on the job, Silver-Tip?" he concluded.

Recovering from his almost thunderstruck amazement the trapper nodded: "To smell out them outlaws' tracks. I'll do 'er. Uh! Hell's Fire! I cayn't walk. Got to use your own hoofs to get down close to the ground an' find sign what cayn't hardly be found."

"No, you can't help me and Kline any now," said

Tedro bitterly. "In a few days it's sure to be too late. Yeh, any minute old Henry's liable to stop a bullet; me the same. . . . Which reminds me, somebody else besides just you, me and Kline had better learn what we know. Truesdale nor none of his pack'll suspect you yet, Joe. You help us now by taking a letter to—" the cowboy paused, rolled a cigarette thoughtfully, concluded: "To Ray Thomas."

"Jake," approved Silver-Tip wagging his head. "Write 'er, kid, so that ink-slinger'll be sure it comes from you and ain't just my gab. . . . I re'lize plenty you can't go to town with me, but where you headin' out to, Tedro?"

"That depends on you, Silver-Tip. You know these mountains better than any man living. Now where, if you was an outlaw, would you pick a hideout that would be safe?"

The trapper pulled his whiskers and squinted south to the distant peaks. "There's a place, kid, down there," pointing, "that'd be a plumb humdinger. I reckon no white man but me ever found 'er. It's right spang between them two Flame Peaks. Here, I'll draw you a map." In the soil of the dooryard he traced lines with his forefinger.

"Here's your steep-walled li'le basin, with water and grass and wood in 'er. Here's a mountain to the north and 'nother to the south—the two peaks, you see? To the east is a daggoned steep slope leadin' down to the upper canyon of Flame Crick. You can get down that canyon for a couple o' miles, but no more.

It narrers to a gorge with water falls an' rocks, rocks, rocks. Howsoever, if you was climbin' up outa the canyon from the east you'd get into this li'le basin through a kinder notch, a gap, and there's 'nother gap over to the west side of it.

"Go through that un to the west, Tedro, and what you see? Why both them mountains jus' drops away, so a fly couldn't hardly hang to the side of neither one of 'em. If you started slidin' you'd end up in the bottom of a chasm 'bout a thousand feet from where you started. Oh, she's a rough, bear-cat of a country. Yet there's a ledge—a fault in the rock—a layer of it kinder juttin' out—runnin' along the side of South Flame Peak for three hundred yards maybe. Then it just ends and there you are looking down into the dag-goned crevice."

Tedro was attentively following the map. "What's on the other side of this chasm?"

"A high short ridge, 'nother mountain really. A ridge you can get along all jake, and if you could get from the basin to it, you could drift down the west slope of the range."

"So? How wide is it, the chasm?"

Joe squinted one eye. "One place it's only 'bout fifty feet wide at the top. When I found this yere basin I was on that ridge and I throwed my rope 'cross the narrer place, noosin' a rock on the ledge I was tellin' you 'bout. Then I crossed the chasm on my rope, hand over hand and walked along the ledge—wide 'nuff for a hoss, and—"

"Why'd you do that? Couldn't you get to this pocket or basin from the north, south or east easier?"

"Uk-unn. Nope. Look at my map. Flame Peak on the north. Flame Peak on the south. Them peaks can't be climbed up over. You moight get in from the east if you was to drop down into upper Flame Canyon, and then climb out again. I wouldn't try that, 'cause the country atween here and that canyon is tougher'n tough. . . . Tedro, if you was to go to that basin, you get on that west ridge like I did and shinny 'cross the chasm on a rope like I did. But, say, Wolf Whalen ain't holed up in that li'le basin. He couldn't get there from Swiftwater Valley."

"Silver-Tip, men are always findin' ways to get through these mountains and over 'em that ain't been found before, and I know Wolf Whalen rode up into lower Flame Canyon. I want a look at this funny pocket—today."

"Kid," said Silver-Tip solemnly, "I advise you agin it. Your hunch moight be right. But you're a cowpuncher not used to usin' yore own hoofs none. You cayn't ride a hoss down through this gosh-awful savage country, 'count of slide rock, canyons, down timber. You got to tackle it afoot and you wouldn't never make it, not a cowboy as cayn't walk."

"I can hoof it if I have to. I see some moccasins in your shack. I'll borrow them and maybe another rope or two."

"We-el," the trapper eyed the younger man—it seemed to Tedro—admiringly. "Maybe your hunch is right. Maybe them bandits is there. You know when a deer comes to a place it cayn't go through nor over, it goes around. Wolf Whalen couldn't go through that gorge atween upper and lower Flame Creek Canyons. He mebbe went around, heh? If I wasn't lamed I'd go with you. Take a li'le grub. Wrap it in that hunk of white canvas. It'll do to spread over you at night. Take a hatchet, plenty matches, too. And luck to you."

They shook hands. Silver-Tip said, "ged-up" to his mule-horse team and took the road to Swiftwater, to deliver a message and to have a dangerous wound treated. Tedro Ames lingered at the trapper's cabin only long enough to get a bite to eat, to unsaddle and turn loose his horse, to change his boots for moccasins, and to make a small pack which he slung over his shoulders. Then he struck out on what he soon realized was the most difficult, the most dangerous and the hardest job of his life.

Time and again he was tempted to turn back, yet always there was the thought in his mind: Wolf Whalen had come from the mountains to Swiftwater Valley, had headed back that same way, up Flame Creek Canyon, toward Flame Peaks. And Silver-Tip Joe's description of the hidden pocket and the ridge west of the peaks across a narrow chasm intrigued Tedro. From this ridge men could go down the western slope of the range.

"If I was a bandit doin' what Wolf and his gang are doin'," thought the cowpuncher, "I'd fix it for a getaway in that direction. The chasm? I'd bridge it of course." He was mighty glad he'd ridden to see Silver-Tip Joe.

Footsore, every muscle and every bone an ache, he yet forced himself to walk and walk and walk, doggedly on and ever on.

Twilight of that evening, Sunday evening, found him on the ridge, which Silver-Tip had mentioned, in reality a huge mountain, rising above timberline, a barren rocky desolate place at its top, swept bare of fresh fallen snow by a piercing cold wind.

Just as the old trapper had said the ridge lay west of the two Flame Peaks, separated from them by a chasm. And what a chasm, apparently bottomless, its walls so precipitous that it might well have been called a cleft. This was the roughest of rough country. Nature must have been in a savage mood when she heaved and writhed in a molten state giving birth to these mountains.

Tedro Ames felt small, helpless, impotent, a tiny human thing of no more consequence than an ant, as he sat down in the shelter of a boulder to rest. Must get up and push on to find the narrow place to throw his rope across and walk it hand over hand to—Abruptly he sucked in his breath, and held it. He had been about to light a cigarette and his hand paused in mid air. The last rays of the departing sun had caught and reflected the glint of metal yonder across the chasm in a nest of boulders just above a narrow gap between those peaks.

Tedro focused his gaze, his eyes drawing to pin-points. He saw the barrel of the rifle that had caught the sun's rays. He saw a man's hat. There was a sentry posted there among the rocks. Tedro knew exulta-tion—and despair. He had found Wolf Whalen's hideout, but a rifleman guarded the west entrance to the basin. Pure luck that the cowboy had halted this far away so the fellow had not seen him.

If Tedro moved farther south along the ridge he would be seen and shot. The sentry was too well entrenched for the cowpuncher to hit him with his Colt, the only weapon he had brought along. Or with a rifle, for that matter. The fellow held a natural fort. The chasm here—some three hundred yards north of the sentry—was too wide to throw a rope across. Nothing on the other side to noose, and nothing for a man to hold to should he get over there; nothing except a sheer wall of rock.

Therefore Tedro could not get at the guard from the rear. However, why should he want to get across the chasm and into the basin? The thing to do was back-track, get help. Backtrack? Why he couldn't walk another mile tonight to save his life, not even to save Sandy McKenzie's life. He was simply used up, done, all-in.

Removing the little pack from his shoulders he rested his head on it and lay sheltered from the cold wind by the huge boulder. The stars came out seem-ingly so very close to earth here above timberline, and the clouds gathered, the wind moaned and still Tedro lay inert, relaxed, too tired to eat, not daring to smoke. How good to rest, rest, rest!

He must have dozed, for suddenly he became aware of being chilled to the marrow, and the stars were now cloud hidden. Ah, 'twas so dark that sentry could no longer see him if he moved. Slowly, painfully southward along the ridge, feeling his way, the cowpuncher walked. If he slipped and rolled into the pitfall at his left, that would be all for Tedro Ames in this world. Would Sandy McKenzie, bright-eyed, winsome Sandy care?

He passed the little notch above which he knew a man stood guard though he could not see him. A reddish reflection shone through the narrow gap itself, indicating a fire in the basin. A fire when Tedro's teeth were chattering! Across the chasm he could make out the ledge, a fault in the rock wall on the side of South Flame Peak. It was a white line against the dark rock wall. Why? Because there was snow on the ledge, he suddenly realized. Therefore the guard could and would of course plainly see a man moving along that ledge! Not a chance of Tedro's getting into the basin— unless he could capture the sentry. Yet he went on, seeking that narrow place in the chasm and he found it—bridged!

It was a brand new bridge, three sturdy stringers under it, poles about four feet in length laid across the stringers, a side rail on each side. The farther end of the bridge met the ledge on the side of South Flame Peak.

"They've got it all fixed to make their getaway to the west," whispered Tedro. "Pretty slick. But if I rip this thing out!"

However there was no timber in the vicinity and the outlaws had used all of that which they must have dragged and carried to this spot to construct their bridge. So the cowboy had no pry pole. Furthermore any noise at the structure would bring a bullet from the sentry. Secure in his nest of rocks that fellow commanded the bridge as well as the ledge trail that led to the basin from this west side.

Tedro dared not cross the bridge, to say nothing of exposing himself on the white trail. Shooting at the guard would be futile. The well-protected fellow had every advantage. Just the one man up there in the rocks could hold a dozen at bay on the ledge—or shoot them down.

Consumed though he was with curiosity and an almost overwhelming desire to size up the outlaws' lair, their horses, equipment and the bandits themselves at close range, Tedro Ames yet realized this was out of the question. Plain suicide and nothing else to venture along the ledge—or even to cross the bridge.

He squatted in the shadow of a large boulder that stood on the rim—such a rock as an efficient cowboy might drop a rope over from the opposite side of the crevice—to think matters out. Opening his pack, he took from it a lariat and a dozen stout buckskin strings, garnered from Silver-Tip Joe's cabin. The strings Tedro tucked into his belt; the rope he hung over his shoulders, then munched on a biscuit and beef sandwich and wished he had a quart of coffee, or at least some water.

No need to hurry with this meal. He was safe against the background of dark earth and rocks on his side of the chasm. But what to do, single-handed? Was he utterly helpless? Would he have to retrace his steps? Aha! But wouldn't Harmon Truesdale and his Black Aces be on the run soon? If so, this was the route they'd take.

"And here's where I stay," whispered Tedro. "I'll rip out the bridge and stop 'em from high-tailin' this way. . . . Oh, yeah? How can I tear up the bridge when that darned sentry—"

He leaped to his feet, all attention. From within the outlaw basin had sounded a loud shout. Other voices were raised. Evidently there was some great excitement. The cowpuncher could not distinguish the words. But his eyes were so accustomed to the darkness that he could see fairly well, and yonder just beyond and above the narrow gap—the west entrance to the pocket—the guard had popped up like a jack-in-the-box into full view. From his place that fellow could not see into the basin, and it was at once evident that he wished to do so.

Tedro's Colt slid out of its holster, to be aimed at the troublesome sentry. But he did not fire. The guard was scrambling down the massed boulders from his rock nest. The fellow could have climbed upward over a

206

parapet from the top of which he could, undoubtedly, have looked down into the pocket. But he preferred to descend from his eyrie—which suited Tedro. Another instant and the cowboy saw him clearly at the mouth of the gap through which shone the rosy, cheery glow of firelight, and the man's entire attention was focused upon something going on within the outlaw hideout!

Like a phantom Tedro Ames crossed the bridge and raced along the narrow, snow-coated ledge; a sheer jump off at his left, an unscalable wall of rock at his right. His moccasin clad feet made no sound. Now he was thirty feet from the guard, and his rope was in his hands. But there wasn't room here to handle a rope. He'd—

Through the notch came excited words that were at last distinct and clear. They crashed on Tedro's ears: "Why this jigger's a gal. More'n just a gal. It's Fay McKenzie of the Half Moon!"

Involuntarily, Tedro uttered a low cry himself. The sentry pivoted, jerked up his Winchester, opened his lips to yell—and a human cyclone struck him.

Next instant the guard reeled drunkenly, dazedly, his rifle falling, his arms waving wildly. Tedro clutched at him, but his hands caught only empty air as the man vanished over the rim! Tedro Ames was alone on the ledge outside the outlaws' lair!

CHAPTER FOURTEEN
THE BLACK ACES GATHER

After Fay McKenzie had been identified and named, by the camp fire in the outlaws' lair there followed a moment of stunned silence, in which all present heard a peculiar noise—hard to identify—coming from the west exit of their hideout. One bandit stepped toward the gap, called: "Anything haywire, Drake?"

"Nope," came a grunted reply. "Jus' a-lookin'."

"Well you're shore gettin' an eyeful," and the outlaw returned to the fire.

"Aw it can't be a girl," Fuzzy burst out. "No girl could ha'—"

"Could ha' downed you an' tied you up and took yore hoss, huh?" Blazer cut in, favoring the youth with a look of sardonic glee. "Well, this un shore done it and us real men'll give you the hoss laugh fer the rest o' yore days, Fuzzy. Ha-haw!"

"Yah," snarled Fuzzy, "you'd a-been downed, too, if you'd been roped round your dirty neck. Laugh will you? I'll jus' take the hide offen yore black-hearted carcass right—"

"Cut it out, both of you!" snapped Wolf. "No fightin'. Fuzzy got hisself tied up by a gal, an' we ain't likely to forget it, nor is he. Terrible blow to a doughty young he-bandit's pride, huh? But, fellers, Fuzzy got hisself loose muy pronto and come to warn us and we catched the spy. Mebbe no harm's done. . . . Miz McKenzie, who was with you? Who knows what you intended doin' and did?"

"Tell 'em to go t' hell, Sandy," grated Ike Bowlaigs.

Wolf turned savagely on the old timer. "Button yore lips. I'm reminded I was on the point o' killin' you, Ike Bowlaigs. 'Course you never put no pizen in our chuck. You didn't have none. But I've taken a-plenty of lip from you already."

"Yah," retorted Ike. "I s'pose when you got a pris'ner you expect him tuh get down on his paws and cringe like a whipped cur every time you come nigh. I s'pose you'd like a feller tuh say, 'Mister Whalen' or 'sir' or 'chief', but me, I called you jus' what you is some several times and I'd do 'er agin right now if a lady wasn't yere, you cross atween a yella-bellied coyote and a nester's bob-wire fence."

"Tie that old coot and plug his mouth, boys," barked Wolf.

Three husky bandits sprang to obey this order. Ensued a brief, fierce tussle, but Ike was soon smothered under the weight of numbers.

"Fix 'im so he can't crawl ner even wiggle," commanded the chief, "and drag him over there agin' the bank away from the fire. Let him half freeze to death. It don't matter. We're a-goin' to heave him over the rim o' the west trail, afore we leave here, and listen for him to hit bottom."

West trail! Fay's interest, since she could do nothing whatever for gritty old Ike, centered on the words.

209

Then there was another exit to this pocket lying between the Flame Peaks. If only she had known that she might have escaped. Too late for regrets now. Her adventure had turned out disastrously and far from accomplishing anything toward rounding up the Black Aces she had succeeded only in placing herself absolutely at their mercy. She knew defeat in its bitterest sense.

What would her mother think? Her father? The loyal Half Moon cowboys? And what would Tedro think and do? This seemed more important than all the rest, and the thought of never, never seeing the curly-headed twinkling-eyed ranny again was harder to bear than all the rest. For she would never see him again on this earth. These outlaws—what a tough, villainous and utterly repulsive lot they were, Wolf himself the personification of Fay's idea of the devil—would not release her. As to what her lot might be—she shuddered and closed her eyes.

"Oh, yes, Miz McKenzie," Wolf resumed, "we got a way o' gettin' outa here to the western slope o' the range. You don't catch this wary old bandit bottlin' himself in a pocket where there's only one way in or out." He told her of the eyebrow trail.

The other bandits had fallen to on the food cooked by Ike. Some of them were hoorawing Fuzzy about his escapade. He glowered at them answering no word, still infuriated. He glowered also at pretty Fay. However she much preferred such a vindictive glare to the bold and ogling glances of others of the villainous crew. In fact the look in Blazer's eyes made her blood run cold. Yet, she reassured herself, there was safety in numbers.

The swarthy, hook-nosed outlaw chief grinned at her: "Miz McKenzie, you ain't answered my questions yet."

"Thar wasn't nobody with her," Fuzzy spoke up. "You can rest easy on that score, boss."

Wolf deftly rolled a cigarette, stood surveying the girl, seated on the hard earth, feet stretched out to the fire, the fire so cheery and bright when all else, for her, was dark, portentous and hopeless. "But how come you was prowlin' alone, girl, and got sight of us; got the chance to do what you did? I know you're a range girl, the equal of any man ridin' and ropin' and shootin' too, perhaps, yet—"

"A heap more'n an equal fer some men," chuckled Blazer, turning his wicked eyes full on young Fuzzy.

Instantly the young bandit snatched a stick of twisted wood, leaped over the fire and brought his club down on Blazer's head. Blazer slumped, but Wolf Whalen, galvanizing to action, caught Fuzzy by the shoulder and twisted the club from his grasp. Then the chief held Fuzzy off at arm's length and cuffed his ears as a father would cuff those of an obstinate boy.

"Set down." Wolf gave the fellow a savage shove. Picking himself up Fuzzy sat as ordered, looking sick. Evidently Wolf Whalen's open hand carried a terrific wallop.

Blazer sat up, stared about dazedly. "Whar's that—

?" he began with an oath and reached for his Colt.

"Cut it, or I'll knock yore ears down!" said Wolf, not loudly but with a certain steely timbre to his voice.

"A'right, boss," mumbled Blazer while Fay gazed at the outlaw chief with grudging respect. This man was a leader, a murderous satanic scoundrel, but a leader. Undoubtedly, she thought now, he must be the master mind of the Black Aces. But no. Earlier this eventful evening she had heard him and Blazer and Fuzzy mention someone they called the Big Gun, someone who was higher yet than Wolf Whalen.

Still calmly smoking his cigarette, he again confronted the girl, again addressed her. "You were doin' your prowlin' in the hills all alone?"

Fay cocked her head to one side, an old familiar and unconscious birdlike gesture: "The witness refuses to answer."

The man's black eyes flashed. "Tedro Ames—and damn that jasper, I should ha' shot him dead the day I traded horses with him—wasn't—?"

"You traded horses with Tedro?" Fay was suddenly standing on her feet in her eagerness.

"Shore. Oh, I've moseyed around down in Swiftwater Valley a heap in the daylight—keepin' hid most o' the time 'course. Seen this jasper, Ames, leadin' the swelligantest pinto ever I seen. Thought o' knockin' him outa his saddle and takin' the hoss, but allowed a shot might bring somebody and make my getaway plenty hot. So I jus' up and hit Tedro for a swap and he swapped. Didn't know me from Adam's off ox."

"Which explains something most satisfactorily," said Fay, her eyes glowing. "I knew all the time Tedro couldn't be what they said he was."

Wolf Whalen smiled crookedly: "So? Still mighty int'rested in that bird. . . . Len Stoddard's scheme didn't work, then? He ain't stackin' up so good with you yet?"

"You ask that when I know enough to send Len Stoddard to the gallows? He stopped Ike from reaching Harpoon and had Ike brought here. I overheard you outlaws talking, you see. Len's a Black Ace, so he's a double-crossing—"

"Needn't flare up so, Miz McKenzie. Len ain't double-crossed me, so he'll be the jigger as gets you and decides what tuh do with you, too."

At this the girl's muscles seemed to turn to water. She sat down most abruptly. Wolf's black orbs devoured her calculatingly for a moment then he turned and found a clean tin plate, placed thereon a portion of a delectable stew which was smoking hot in a huge black kettle beside the fire. He poured out a cup of coffee, selected a golden brown biscuit from a Dutch oven and brought this meal to Fay. Ike Bowlaigs doubtless hated cooking for the bandits, but he had done his job well. Perhaps, in spite of his brash talk to the chief, he had hoped they would delay murdering him.

"Here you are. I been neglectin' my guest," said Wolf in a softer tone than he had as yet employed. The tone of a man, be he hard-bitten or otherwise, who has suddenly discovered that he himself is smitten by the charm of a girl.

Fay realized this subtle change instantly, and shuddered. Small choice between this renegade and Len Stoddard, yet of the two Wolf was the better, for he was no hypocrite. Avowedly wicked and ruthless, a thief and a killer, he made no pretense of being anything else. She accepted the plate and cup, and, in spite of her predicament, soon found that she had an appetite; was ravenously hungry.

The swarthy bandit squatted on his spurred heels a little to one side so that the firelight shone directly upon her sweet oval face. He rolled another cigarette, puffed reflectively for a few moments and said: "So you know jus' what Len Stoddard is? Like several other gents in the valley he figgered he'd never be found out, so he'd be settin' pretty when all the hell raisin' was over and the fire had burnt out and the smoke had rolled away."

Fay sampled the meat in the stew—mountain sheep and delicious. The outlaw was leading up to something. She'd let him talk, and wasn't this the experience of a lifetime—if only one might live to tell about it. The walled basin, the horses in it grazing as naturally and unconcernedly as any roundup cavvy. The sentry yonder on his pinnacle, invisible from the fire, and the narrow gap between him and beyond that the sharp descent to Upper Flame Canyon. The fire, the dirty and whisker-stubbled and bearded bandits around it, their small tent, their scattered beds, their saddles and their rifles near at hand. Beyond the circle of firelight in the deep shadow of the steep bank poor, loyal old Ike tied hard and fast and cruelly gagged. And here in the center of all this under the cloud-strewn sky with only a few wan stars twinkling down upon the scene was Fay herself. The girl of the Half Moon unwilling guest of Wolf Whalen, bandit chief. He was speaking again:

"The last definite and authentic report I had, as to whether or not Len Stoddard and the rest of 'em in the deal would be settin' pretty depended on killin' Tedro Ames deader than a door nail."

Fay swallowed hard and took a sip of coffee to keep from choking. Wolf continued: "And that before that troublesome jasper had a chance to spill what he knows to square men who'd believe him. However, you've learned a heap yourself and it's a cinch Len Stoddard ain't goin' to get no place with you. Such bein' the case, you mighty classy filly, wouldn't you rather throw in with me than him?"

With difficulty Fay retained her composure and forced herself to remain seated. She kept her hot eyes on her plate.

"Needn't answer now," the bandit resumed. "But think this over. I wouldn't tell it if you didn't know already how Len's a plumb rotten egg and one of the Black Aces. He had his brother, Jake, murder Ab Thurston."

Fay's startled eyes met those of Wolf Whalen. "You —you're clearing Tedro of that accusation. Not that I ever thought he did it. But why—why did the Stoddards murder their own foreman? I've heard that Thurston was wearing Tedro's big white Stetson that night and I drew the inference that the bullet was surely intended for Tedro."

Wolf blew smoke through his high bridged nose and shrugged. " 'Twasn't. There was no mistake 'bout it, though God knows Len and Jake must have wished a hundred times since that night—not so long ago—that they'd murdered Tedro Ames as well as Thurston.

"This Ab Thurston was a square shooter. Len sounded him out on the Black Ace deal without mentionin' anything definite. Just enough so Thurston'd realize there was some mighty dirty crooked work on tap. Ab told Len where to head in and Len and Jake figured Ab knew too much for them to be safe once the Black Ace game began in earnest.

"Len had another ax to grind beside just eliminatin' his foreman. He allowed—with good reasons, too—that Tedro Ames was ridin' top hoss with the daughter of the Half Moon. Len was nuts about you, Miz McKenzie, still is. If Tedro Ames could be branded a murderer, that ought to turn Fay McKenzie against him; ought to give Len Stoddard a clear field—so Len figured. And that's the truth of why and how Ab Thurston died and how Tedro Ames was framed.

"Remember you ain't goin' to be allowed to go home. You know too much. Now, won't you throw in with me 'stead of Len?"

Wolf bent towards the girl, fire in his black eyes, and at last his hand reached out, gripped her arm. She looked at this hand, slim fingered, deft, capable, the hand of a gunfighter—a killer—and she recoiled as though from a snake. But she was spared the necessity of answering the bandit with words, for at this moment sounds from the eastern entrance floated into the little walled basin. The sound of many hoofs on the rocky soil. The sentry's sharp challenge:

"Password?"

"Lobos."

The sentry's voice again. "I knowed it was you fellers afore you ever clumb up outa the canyon. Ride on, Mr. Truesdale, you and yore men."

"Truesdale!" echoed Fay. This was the first she had known of the banker's connection with the dread Black Aces.

The outlaws had all grabbed their rifles and leaped away from the fire. Now as they returned, up into the pocket and on to the circle of firelight rode the big, dignified white-haired, white-mustached Harmon Truesdale. Fay saw him with new eyes, this great man she had trusted, the man to whom all Swiftwater town and Swiftwater Valley looked up and trusted. Behind him, all in a bunch, like crowding cattle rode Len and Jake Stoddard, the lanky, peanut-headed Greasy Holderness, Boyd Loomis, Mooch the bar-fly, and two strangers to Fay. Tight-lipped, cold-eyed fellows, just to look at them caused cold shivers to run down the girl's back. Instinctively she knew they were gunmen

217

—the killers of the Black Ace crew, who shot men from ambush.

Every newcomer's face registered amazement at sight of Fay McKenzie. Len Stoddard, out of his saddle in a twinkling, started to run to her side, changed his mind, and halted confronting Wolf Whalen. Glowering at the swarthy bandit with murder in his eyes, he snapped:

"Who told you and yore scum of hell crew to bring her here?"

"Cool your hot head with a hunk of snow from Flame Peak," retorted Wolf entirely unruffled. "She came of her own free will. Ye-ah, this gritty girl, alone, smelt out the outlaw trail."

"Alone?" asked Truesdale quickly.

Fay saw his heavy features and his eyes clearly in the bright firelight, and felt shock at the change in him. Heretofore this man had always seemed as imperturbable as the Rocky Mountains, calm eyed, reserved, his face poker-masked. But now his features were haggard, his eyes sunken into their sockets and burning with what seemed an unquenchable fire.

"Alone?" he iterated. "That—" he choked. "That Tedro Ames wasn't with her?"

"No," said Wolf Whalen. "This means you ain't—"

"Found him? Killed him? *No!*"

Truesdale's voice, hoarse, unnatural, filled with blind fury told Fay that Tedro—her Tedro or was he? She'd sent him away—was the reason for this change in Truesdale, for his fury. A sentence uttered by

218

Blazer, earlier tonight and overheard by the girl ran through her mind. "Tedro Ames has got the Big Gun clawin' out his hair." At last she knew the Big Gun— Harmon Truesdale.

"And that's not all," spoke up Boyd Loomis. "Henry Kline, I hope he rots in hell, and Ray Thomas, I'd like to drown him in his own ink, are wise to us, too. We had Kline in jail, aimed to lynch him t'night. Thomas took him out. They got away. Kline nicked Jake with a bullet and kilt a hoss for us. Atter that, the las' we seen o' him and the inky editor they was foggin' north."

"Good for Henry Kline!" thought Fay, clapping her hands. "And Tedro hasn't been caught!"

"Swing down and rest your saddles," invited Wolf. "Why ain't you still huntin' for Kline, Thomas, and this hell-twister, Ames?"

"I've had these hired assassins," Truesdale glared at the two tight-lipped men of his party, "gunning for Tedro since the night he stole Charon. They've bungled the job."

Wolf looked at him slant-eyed. "But Tedro slipped outa your hands after I helped grab him on Wind Ridge. . . . Did some bunglin' yourself, Banker Truesdale, especially havin' *that ten thousand bucks tied on your saddle* on Charon that night at Kline's ranch."

Fay, all interest, wished she knew what they were talking about.

"Rub it in, Mister Outlaw," rasped Truesdale. "Damn! I've cursed myself about it and I've cursed

Tedro Ames. He's preyed on my mind 'til I'm almost a raving maniac," the banker of Swiftwater plunged on vehemently. "Due to that cowboy-rancher, known as happy-go-lucky, thriftless, good-for-nothing and considered harmless, the whole scheme—and I still maintain it was an excellent scheme—has backfired on me with a terrific wallop."

"Ye-ah, it looked like a good scheme to me," said Wolf calmly, "or I wouldn't have throwed in with you."

"'Twas!" snapped Truesdale. "I didn't see a chance for it to fail, because I, Len and Jake, Loomis, Holderness, Greenwald, were all reliable citizens, trusted men that no finger of suspicion would ever point to."

Wolf nodded. "Right. But the first sock on the jaw was when Arch Greenwald didn't get that big wad from the girl of the Half Moon." He turned and addressed Fay: "You see, loss of that jack would have forced you to return to the bank and borrow another twenty thousand smackers, Miz McKenzie. 'Course Mister Truesdale allowed old Bill would sure settle his daughter's notes in due time. But Tedro Ames plunked a bullet into Greenwald and—"

Harmon Truesdale burst into violent profanity. Controlling himself, he gritted: "If it hadn't been that the Half Moon ranch is cursed with dogs, which would have sounded the alarm, I'd have had somebody get that twenty thousand before Sandy McKenzie took it to the rendezvous." Another oath.

Fay thought: "I can be thankful we have our collies.

Too bad I'll never, never have a chance to tell these things I'm learning!"

Wolf Whalen favored the banker with a sardonic smile: "Such language from the dignified mayor and first citizen of Swiftwater," he remarked. "Console yourself, Mr. Truesdale, by rememberin' how two of our men will certain-sure rob old Bill McKenzie of the dough he gets for his beef at Kansas City—a good, fat wad, too."

"Yes," said Truesdale. "Yes. That's one small comfort. But do you realize that—with one other exception —the cash we have collected from ranchers and others is all money I advanced to them?"

Judging from the outlaw chief's expression Fay thought he was finding a sort of satanic amusement in the situation: "Uh-huh," he returned. "That one exception was Rawley, the saloon man. Well, that fourteen thousand bucks ain't to be sneezed at. . . . Miz McKenzie, our banker friend aimed to take a nice juicy cut outa all the dough his Black Aces collected from ranchers—us fellers to split the balance—and then Truesdale'd feather his nest proper when the cowmen and others—all grateful to him for helpin' 'em out, savin' 'em from death at the hands of the Black Aces in fact—paid their obligations to him.

"He holds a flock o' notes and mortgages now, but can't collect on 'em 'cause the fire's been put under him. Plumb ironical, eh, Mister Banker?"

"Ironical? That's a good word," Truesdale said with brittle emphasis. "Instead of having my dream come true, I've become almost a penniless fugitive; a man on the dodge with a hungry noose waiting for me—if I'm caught. And it's all due to just one man, that double-damned Tedro Ames! The scoundrel got away with the ten thousand dollars that was on my saddle that night at the H K ranch—the money I'd advanced Kline. At least we've never recovered it. He, that—"

"Hey, boss," called Greasy Holderness, "don't give Tedro all the credit for bustin' us up. 'Member that U. S. Marshal done—"

"Hell!" snorted Truesdale, smacking his right fist against the palm of his other hand. "Marshal Ormsdale was never dangerous, not more so than the brainless chump, Sheriff Potter. I took long chances on Potter. He might have tumbled, but he never did. I took no chances with Ormsdale. He was in town where we could watch his every move and keep tabs on him."

"Yet he was a clever jasper," Holderness persisted. "Wolf, this marshal figgered out somethin' Truesdale thunk never could be figgered out. At the hotel Ormsdale works over stuff Postmaster Jim gave him 'til three in the mornin' then on the Q. T. he puts a fat envelope in Harry Ayres' safe to the hotel. Me and Jake Stoddard gets that envelope. In it is the evidence and a letter to the sheriff of Harpoon. A letter Ormsdale must ha' figgered to mail in the mornin'. He names the man what writ the Black Ace threats and he wants this Harpoon sheriff to come pronto with a big posse to help him."

222

"And who'd this Ormsdale name?" asked Wolf.

With his thumb Greasy Holderness indicated Harmon Truesdale.

"How could he have found out?" the banker yammered. "I used my left hand and I practiced the peculiar small penmanship for over a year."

"I dunno how he done it," Holderness shrugged. "But, me an' Jake Stoddard—Jake mostly—settled Ormsdale's hash afore he had no chance to talk."

"So?" said the bandit chief. "Yet that ink-spillin' Thomas and Kline know a-plenty and will be settin' the hull valley afire for you jaspers, and us, pronto."

"I said as much earlier," the banker snapped. "And if Sandy McKenzie could find your trail, Wolf Whalen, somebody else soon will. Let's go."

"We'll split the swag afore we leave," Wolf stated decisively.

All of Truesdale's party had dismounted. Some were making fresh coffee and finishing up the food already cooked. One outlaw had begun to pack the camp outfit; another was taking down the tent. Two more, having led up a couple of horses, were loading beds upon these.

At Wolf's order a bandit now spread a tarpaulin near the fire. On this Wolf and Truesdale piled sacks of cash, money belts and wallets, then sitting opposite each other they began to count the money.

Len Stoddard joined Fay. Regardless of the freezing stare he received from her bright eyes he began: "The deal's gone just as haywire for me as for Truesdale. I

223

can take it on the chin better'n he can, though. 'Course I wish the scheme had come out hunkydory; wish you hadn't found out what you have. Howsoever, regardless o' any ideas you may have you're goin' with me."

Offering no reply, the girl thought: "We'll leave by way of the eyebrow trail Wolf told me of—a ledge wide enough for one horse, on one side of the mountain, on the other a sheer jump-off. I'll lie to them and say I'll go willingly, so they won't tie me, but I wonder if Tedro, Mother, Daddy or anybody will ever find all that's left of Sandy away down in the bottom of the chasm?"

Tedro? Where was he? Somehow she hoped he'd appear. But what could he do if he did? And it was simply ridiculous to hope. How about Kline and Thomas who had escaped from Truesdale's killers earlier this night? If Kline got a bunch of men together and found the outlaw trail he could not possibly follow it in the dark. As for the Half Moon cowboys, even though she had sent Scottie home with a message, she now had no hope of any help from that source. Furthermore, her father, unwarned because Ike had failed to reach Harpoon, would be robbed—perhaps murdered.

No hope of anything, really. Ike Bowlaigs, tied and gagged, could do nothing. There were—she counted the men present—fifteen. The sentry at the east entrance made sixteen. There was one at the west exit, too. Shortly after Fay had been caught she had heard this fellow addressed as Drake. So there must be seventeen men in all, and certainly no one man could do anything against this tough crew.

Suddenly the cold, still air carried a faint sound to the hopeless girl's ears. Steadily it grew louder. It was the sound of many horses in the rocky canyon east of this little basin. Men—a good many men—were coming up the outlaw trail!

Of course the bandits had heard. All work had ceased. The men were still figures as they listened. Across the little pocket floated the plaintive call of a night hawk.

"What's that?" asked Truesdale tensely.

Wolf had bounded to his feet at the first sound: "Our sentry warnin' us," he returned in a low tone. Then, without raising his voice: "Your rifles, boys. Plenty shells. All our gang is here. No friends of ourn can be ridin' up outa Flame Canyon.

"Jake Stoddard, you got a crippled shoulder, stay and ride herd on the gal and Ike Bowlaigs. All the rest follow me. We'll spread out like a big fan on the slope above them fellers, hide behind rocks, let 'em get close, then pour a crossfire into 'em from two sides. From in front as well."

"Annihilate them!" ejaculated Truesdale. "A massacre!"

CHAPTER FIFTEEN

THE EYEBROW TRAIL

The boss outlaw was not lingering to listen to Truesdale. Followed by a dozen men, all armed with rifles, he sped down the pocket, eastward, and vanished from Fay's sight. But, for some reason, Harmon Truesdale stayed at the camp with Jake Stoddard.

The girl's mind was a tumult. Though her heart pounded wildly, her body felt as if ice flowed through her veins. Those horsemen, coming up the steep slope from Flame Canyon, must be her friends, Henry Kline, Ray Thomas, ranchers, Tedro! Unwittingly they were riding into an ambush, and what an ambush. Truesdale had said with grim exultation, "A massacre." It would be just that, unless—

Fay's smoldering eyes darted to the saddled and packed horses, still near the fire. She'd jump on one and—

"No you don't!" snapped Truesdale as if he had read her mind. "Sit down!"

He was in front of her, blocking her path. She dodged to the right, tried to win past him. The man caught her by one arm and one shoulder, spun her about and gave her a violent shove that sent her sprawling.

"Lie there," rasped Truesdale, standing menacingly over the girl's figure. "Tell me something, quick. Is

Tedro Ames with that bunch?" pointing east with one hand. "Tedro was sweet on you. It stands to reason you can tell me where—?"

"Right here in person to answer!" spoke a voice which sent electric tingles along Fay's nerves.

Lifting her head and shoulders, she saw that which she would never forget to her dying day—Tedro Ames face to face with Harmon Truesdale!

Yet, could it be, or was she dreaming? Certainly the ragged, torn and very dirty jumper and overalls and the tattered moccasins were such attire as she had never seen dressy Tedro wearing. But the slouchy old black hat she had seen once before, on the day when the cowboy had interrupted a holdup and shot Arch Greenwald. And she had just heard Tedro's voice.

No, she was not dreaming. Truesdale was seeing what she saw, and blood rushed to his big face, turning it black so great was his rage. He leaped backwards tugging at his gun, and with a savage, unholy joy Tedro sprang to the attack. Smashing fists rained blows on the banker's breast and stomach and face. His Colt, half-drawn, went spinning aside. He tried to cry out and a fist closed his mouth; another drove to his chin. The ground caught his body.

Tedro had spoken only the once. Thereafter he had been a raging whirlwind. Not the deliberate, twinkling-eyed Tedro Fay had known, but a grim-jawed fighting man with a fierce gleam in his eyes and all the savageness of a wolf at bay. Now he jerked buckskin strings from his belt, stooped over Truesdale, tied and gagged the man with desperate haste, and then, with just one glance at Fay, he was gone—gone to the horses nearby.

The girl suddenly remembered Jake Stoddard. Where was he? Jake would get his gun and— Why, another fight was going on! Across the fire from Fay, Ike Bowlaigs and Jake Stoddard were at each other's throats. Jake, she had heard, was wounded, yet he had shown scarcely any sign of it, and he certainly wasn't now. He was a husky brute. Surely such an old fellow as Ike couldn't— But, ducking under a haymaker from Jake, Ike rammed the man in the stomach head on. As Jake folded up, landing on his back, Ike pounced upon him.

So swift this action, both Tedro's fight and Ike's, that the astounded girl had not yet scrambled to her feet. Her gaze flicked from Ike Bowlaigs to find Tedro. There he was among the saddled horses. She saw him jerk bridles from three of these and deftly tie those bridles to the animals' tails. He waved his battered old hat at the already startled horses. They whirled, snorted as the dangling bridles hit their heels, kicked wildly and were off, running like scared coyotes.

Fay heard them tornado through the narrow gap at the east of the basin, and, an instant later, with thump and ring of hoofs, the three terrified horses plunged down the rocky slope into Upper Flame Canyon. Dumbfounded questions and lurid oaths told of the outlaws' dismayed chagrin. By stampeding the horses

Tedro had warned the riders coming up the canyon; had wrecked the Black Ace ambush!

Loose rocks rolled and rumbled as the horses cascaded onward and suddenly the night was split wide open with the crash of rifle-fire. The thwarted bandit crew were shooting, but, Fay ventured to hope, uselessly. Abruptly Tedro Ames was beside her. He caught her wrist, lifted her erect and held her close for an unforgettable instant when she would gladly have clung to him. But he swept her up in his arms and ran past the fire to the base of the cliff where Ike had been tied. A rope dangled there.

Setting Fay on her feet, Tedro said: "Climb. Wait for us on top," and was gone.

She gripped the rope, waiting. She didn't want to climb anywhere without him or leave him ever. What was he—? He was beside her again, burdened with a couple of rifles and dragging Harmon Truesdale. Old Ike was coming, too, with a heavy burden—Jake Stoddard.

"Up, Sandy! Hurry!"

She saw the need of haste. Wolf Whalen and his crew were already swarming back into the basin. Fay went up the slender cord without knowing how she did it. Tedro was right behind her, giving her a boost to the top of a rock parapet and calling under his breath: "Careful. This is powerful narrow."

In the dim light she saw he had tied buckskin strings to the rifles and looped them about his neck. He had another rope also. Now, above the basin on a narrow

229

shelf, he laid down the rifles, looped his rope around a rock and dropped its end over the rim. A minute later, Ike came scrambling upward and Tedro gave him a lift. Before leaving the basin, Ike had tied one rope around Truesdale, the other to Jake Stoddard.

Now Tedro and the old hand turned their attention to the ropes, began to pull on one. Realizing what they were doing, Fay sprang to help them.

The three dragged Harmon Truesdale up out of the pocket. Tedro grabbed the man and slid his body down the western side of the parapet and left him in a nest of jumbled rocks. Then Fay, Ike and Tedro pulled on the second rope, hoisting Jake Stoddard up the incline.

They were not an instant too soon. Wolf Whalen, his bandits and Truesdale's henchmen had reached the fire. Wolf called an order:

"Get all the hosses that's left together and saddle quick. . . . What popped anyhow? You s'pose that girl spooked them three broncs?"

"Don't know," panted Len Stoddard. "But it certainly foiled our ambush. Those cowboys or whoever they are in the canyon turned back and I don't think our lead hit any of 'em."

"Thank God!" breathed Tedro, his lips close to Fay's cheek. "It's Kline and the Half Moon punchers. They'd have been mowed down if—"

"Tedro, it couldn't be our Half Moon cowboys. For Ike didn't get to Harpoon."

"I found that out, sent another man. Listen."

In the basin Wolf Whalen yelled: "They're gone.

The girl and Ike both!"

"And where's Truesdale and Jake?" gasped Stoddard.

"Where?" echoed Wolf. "None of 'em could ha' slipped out to the east or climbed out. . . . I get it! I told the girl about our west trail 'long the side o' the mountain. She must ha' got Ike loose someway. The two of 'em are leggin' it along that trail, Jake and Truesdale hot after 'em."

"But they couldn't ha'!" gasped Blazer. "Our sentry, Drake. You forget him?" With this Blazer plunged through the notch that opened to the west.

"Drake!" he bellowed. "Drake!" There was no reply.

Blazer returned to the fire. "Chief, somehow they got our sentry. Must ha' took him with 'em or chucked him over the rim."

"Likely," snarled Wolf. "Though I dunno how a gal and an ol' man could have done it. Yet I rec'lect as Drake come down from his post, earlier t'night t' look in here, when he hadn't ought to have."

Men were rushing to the fire with saddled horses. One shouted: "Let's get out while the goin's good."

"Let's," agreed Wolf. Then: "Where's that cash?"

All eyes turned to the tarpaulin still lying close to the fire. The money was gone! On the narrow perch above the hideout Fay gripped Tedro's arm tightly. "Cowboy, how'd you hide that money when you were moving like double-greased lightning?"

"I scooped it up and flipped it into a Dutch oven not

231

far from the fire and slapped the lid on the oven."

Ike chuckled softly: "Sandy, ain't he the goldarn-dest, go-gettin'est jasper ever you seen? He's got 'em panicked plumb! Fust I knowed he was 'round, sump'n drops down close tuh me and I makes out it's a rope, an' then thar's Tedro hisself. He had me untied more'n half an hour ago, so I got over bein' numb. We was waitin' for a break, and when we got one—Say when you crowd one o' them easy-goin' fellers like o' Tedro, get him smoky, you start somethin'!"

Fay gripped the veteran's horny hand wordlessly. She was watching what was going on in the basin. A brief search for the missing money had failed and Blazer snarled: "Somethin' danged spooky 'bout all this. We goin' tuh be forced tuh lam out without no jack?"

"It's that blankety-blanked Truesdale pullin' a double-cross!" snapped Wolf. "Never trust a banker!" Then: "Where's that sentry as was on the east side? . . . Hey, Stivers, you was on duty a-lookin' out when we laid our ambush. Didn't you see what happened here, by the fire?"

"Gosh-darn it, Chief, I was watchin' the east slope all the time—lookin' for them fellers to come in sight up the canyon. I'm danged sorry—but I seen nothin' here."

This reply brought a storm of oaths from the Black Ace bandits. But Tedro whispered: "I'm a heap relieved to hear that. The guard over there had me bothered plenty."

"Hit leather, boys, and take the eyebrow trail," roared Wolf. "They must ha' gone that way. Ha! We'll rip out the chasm bridge behint us. That'll stop any pursuit!"

Bounding to his saddle the chief led the way through the narrow notch to the ledge trail that hung on the side of South Flame Mountain. On the parapet Fay gripped Ike's hand the tighter:

"Ike, they're going to escape after all the terrible things they've done."

"Oh, maybe not escape," whispered Tedro Ames.

"Tedro, what did you do to the sentry who was on this west side? I know there was one."

"I didn't want him to page me to Wolf and his nice guests, so I tapped him gently with both fists. . . . Pick up that rifle, Ike, old horse. Follow me."

Tedro had snatched the second rifle himself and was leading the precarious way down the rocky slope, westward. Fay held to his left arm: "'Gently?'" she iterated. "Oh, yes? As gently as you hit Truesdale? Tedro you're becoming a terribly rough—"

Further words were cut off as they slid down jumbled rocks past where Truesdale and Jake were now hidden to arrive at a little nest-like place among the boulders. At her right from here Fay saw a yawning abyss; across it a dark ridge. Directly ahead of her, but below this eyrie, a white line ran along the side of South Flame Peak. This was the eyebrow trail. Men were riding slowly in single file along it—the bandits or Black Aces.

Abruptly Tedro gripped the girl's shoulders forcing her down, so her head was below the rocks. He crouched himself. Ike was already on his knees, the barrel of his rifle lay in a niche between two rocks. A wild shout ran along the ledge trail. A shout of thunderstruck dismay. Then a voice, high-pitched, unnatural and scared, boomed:

"Hells Fire! Our bridge is out!"

"Tedro! Cowboy lover, you—" Fay's eyes shone in the dim light as she turned her face up toward the puncher's. "You tore out their bridge?"

"Uh-huh. I discovered that when somethin' drops into that black hole you don't ever hear it hit bottom, so I dared to go to work on that bridge using sentry Drake's rifle for a pry pole."

"And the Black Aces on that narrow narrow trail can't climb up or go down!"

"It's even a little worse for 'em than that, Sandy. The trail's so blamed narrow hosses can't turn around on it, and from here one rifleman can command the length of the trail, can stop anybody from tossin' a rope across the chasm even. Black Aces'll be headin' this way, afoot, in a minute. You want to hold 'em on that ledge, Ike?"

"Do I!" whooped the old timer. "Tedro, I shore do. We got them varmints by the tail with a downhill pull!"

Three men, on foot, were hurrying back along the trail, not yet realizing they were trapped. Ike Bowlaigs muttered something about he wished he had old

Topsy, his ancient buffalo gun, but mebbe he could use this un. He squinted along the barrel. Crack! A bullet struck rock just above the first bandit's head and ricochetted with a peculiarly sinister whizzing sound.

The effect upon the three was as if a bolt of lightning had struck directly in front of them. All whirled and scurried back the way they had just come.

"Them tarantulas doan seem tuh like the setup none," chuckled Ike.

"They'll like it less after you hold 'em for a few hours," said Tedro.

"Gosh all tomahawks!" Ike exclaimed. "Looks to me like one smart feller is shakin' him out a Blocker loop in his rope for to try to noose a boulder 'cross the chasm. I got to stop that."

Again his rifle spoke. A loud shriek answered and a man leaping high in the air was only prevented from falling over the rim because two of his companions grabbed him.

"And that's a warnin' to you!" yelled Ike Bowlaigs. "You long-fanged coyotes get gay and I'll pepper them hosses some. Spook 'em 'til they'll tromp you to sausage meat a-tryin' to get away. Say, Wolf Whalen, you killin'-minded sidewinder what made me cook fer you, if any o' your scum-o'-hell mob start throwin' bullets this way *I'll shoot to kill.* Be daggoned careful you mind Papa."

"Lay off!" roared Wolf Whalen. "You jus' kilt Len Stoddard deader'n a nit. Lay off. We're minded to talk turkey with you."

"Just cool your heads and heels, think things over for an hour or two or three, fellers," shouted Tedro. "We'll have more men, in a little bit, to welcome you, one at a time, back to outlaws' pocket."

"Wolf," squealed Greasy Holderness, "that's Tedro Ames speakin'. Might ha' guessed he'd be in at the finish. It jus' ain't human the way that feller's been on our trail all a-time."

"Len's the whelp as stopped me from gettin' to Harpoon," said old Ike grimly. "I sure ain't sorry none 'twas him my lead hit."

But Fay McKenzie's face had turned white and Tedro spoke hastily: "Ike can hold 'em. Let's go, Sandy."

He helped the girl to climb back among the rocks, past where Truesdale and Jake Stoddard now lay, both securely tied, to reach the parapet overlooking the little basin. Both of Tedro's ropes, still fastened to rocks, were coiled here. He lowered one, slid down it, followed by Fay. Wordlessly they crossed the open area, went through the east gap and on to the slope above Upper Flame Canyon.

"You call to our friends," said Tedro then.

"Yo-ho, men. It's all right now!" the girl's voice rang high and clear.

"That you, Sandy?" came a tremendously relieved reply.

"Jess Walker!" cried Fay to Tedro. "You were right. It is our rannies!"

"Which means," said the cowboy, "that Slim

Shafter got through to Harpoon. Of course he wired Bill McKenzie to be a-lookin' out, and knowin' your dad like I do, Sandy, I'll say you can rest easy."

"Oh, I'm sure Daddy, forewarned, will be able to take care of himself, Tedro. . . . What's that you're calling, Jess? . . . How do you and Harry Kline and Ray Thomas and the punchers know this isn't a trick? How do you know but what the Black Ace pack are forcing me to say what I said to lead you into another ambush? . . . Um, I don't blame you for being wary. I'd be, too."

"Tedro Ames, speakin'," boomed Tedro. "Kline, you know I wouldn't lie to you. Everything's hunkydory. Come—"

"How the blue blazes can things be hunkydory?" demanded Henry Kline. "Tedro, you don't mean that you and Sandy has got the best of—"

"Climb up here and see," Tedro called.

"Yes," Fay added, "come on, Jess, and you, cowboys. We'll be powerful glad to see you."

She faced the man by her side, gazing up at his face shadowed by his tattered black hat. "Tedro, what're you going to do now the excitement's all over?"

"Hadn't thought much about it, Sandy. Would kinda like to get my little old T A ranch back again and see if I could make a go of it. That is, if—?" he broke off.

"If what, Tedro?" eagerly.

"If—" the cowboy's hands came up and gripped Fay's arms. He pushed her away from him—the better to see her face. "If," he iterated, "I had you to—Sandy, your eyes ain't lying to me? *You do care?*"

"Kiss me, Tedro! Though I don't care if the whole world sees our love, kiss me before the others come."

At this instant cloud curtains lifted from the crests of Flame Peaks and those hoary sentinels of Flame Range seemed to nod at each other and smile.

Stephen Payne was born in North Park, Colorado. He worked as a cowboy and rancher in his early years, supplementing his income beginning in 1924 by writing Western fiction for the magazine market, and sold nearly 900 stories in the course of his career. In the 1930s he began writing Western novels, including *Lawless Range* (1933) that was filmed as *Lawless Range* (Republic, 1935) starring John Wayne and *Black Aces* (1936) that was filmed as *Black Aces* (Universal, 1937) starring Buck Jones. His short story, "Tracks", in *West Magazine* (3/17/28) was the basis for *Swifty* (Diversion, 1935) starring Hoot Gibson. In the 1940s and 1950s, Payne became familiar to British readers in a series of Western novels published by Wright & Brown, including *Lights Out at the Split Y* (1944) and *Trail The Man Down* (1957). Payne also began contributing stories to *Boy's Life* and writing young adult Westerns. His *Young Hero Of The Range* (1954) won a Spur Award from the Western Writers of America. His autobiography was entitled *When The Rockies Ride Hard* (1966), about his boyhood on a North Park ranch. The tone of his Western fiction combines humor with seriousness, a rare mixture that has long delighted readers.